She stiffened at the touch of his arm, but only for a moment.

No man had been that close in four years. How she missed the strength, the security, and the love of a man's protective arm. She relaxed and found herself magnetically drawn to his nearness.

The fire snapped, sparks sizzled, and the room filled with a cozy warmth, but its origin was not the blazing logs; it was generated by the foursome on the sofa. It penetrated their minds, hearts, and bodies as they enjoyed one another's company. Carlee found herself enjoying the closeness a little too much, and it frightened her. She wanted to press herself into Dan's arm, to rest her head on his shoulder, to feel his breath on her hair.

But there was no place in her life for a three-week fling. And she knew there was no place in Dan's life for a woman with a ready-made family, not that he'd be interested in her. What did she have to offer that he couldn't find in any city, any state? No; she was a nothing in his world. How could she even think there might ever be anything between them?

JOYCE LIVINGSTON is a real Kansas "lady" who lives in a little cabin that her husband built overlooking a lake. She is a proud grandmother who retired from television broadcasting, but she keeps very busy lecturing and teaching about quilting and sewing. She is also a part-time tour escort, which takes her to all kinds of fantastic places. *Ice Castle* is her first published novel, but she has had books and articles published on sewing, quilting, crafts, cooking, parenting, travel, personal color, and devotions—you name it.

Ice Castle

Joyce Livingston

Heartsong Presents

A note from the author:

I love to hear from my readers! You may correspond with me by writing:

Joyce Livingston
Author Relations
PO Box 719
Uhrichsville, OH 44683

ISBN 1-57748-697-8

ICE CASTLE

Cover illustration by Victoria Lisi and Julius.

PRINTED IN THE U.S.A.

one

"Which do you like best?"

Carlee Bennett whirled around to find a handsome man standing beside her. He held two colorful containers in his hands and wore a friendly smile. "Spray? Or bottle?"

"Oh, no contest," she quipped with an equally friendly smile. "Spray. That's what I use. I hate those bottles!"

"Hey, thanks for the advice," he replied pleasantly as he placed one of the containers back onto its shelf. "I've never tried the spray stuff, but it sure looks like it might be easier to handle than the bottle of saline I've been using. Am I ever glad someone invented contacts; I'd probably be out of a job without them."

She normally didn't pursue a conversation with a stranger, but he seemed like a nice enough guy and his comment intrigued her. She gave him a quizzical look. "They won't let you wear glasses on your job? What do you do for a living?"

"Skater," he replied casually, as his eyes scanned the fine print on the spray can.

"Skater? What kind of skater?"

"Ice skater. I'm in Kansas City with Ice Fantasy at the Kemper Arena. Our last performance is tonight."

She turned to face him directly. "Really?" she asked in surprise. "I have tickets for tonight's performance. What numbers will you be doing? I'll watch for you."

He took a quick glance at his watch and dropped the spray can into his cart. "Wow! Didn't know it was getting so late. I gotta git. Thanks for the help." With a quick nod and a gorgeous toothy grin that highlighted his deep dimples, he took off down the aisle toward the row of checkout stands lining the front of the big discount store.

She quickly lifted a hand and called out to him. "Wait! You didn't say which parts you'll be skating in the ice show!"

He stopped long enough to turn his head and call back over his shoulder as he moved with haste toward the cash register and the waiting clerk. "Prince Charming! I'll be the guy in the white tights—without glasses!"

❧

At Kemper Arena, Carlee tightened her arms about her daughter's slim shoulders and pulled her close. "Keep watching! Remember what the book said?"

Four-year-old Becca lifted her shining face and smiled at her mother. "The prince will come and wake her up?"

"That's right!"

"That's dumb!" Eight-year-old Bobby clamped his hands over his little sister's eyes and grinned at his mom, who instantly pulled his hands away from the little girl's face.

"Bobby, stop! I wanna see the prince!" Becca buried her face in her mother's neck. "Mama, make him stop!"

For several weeks now the young mother had been excited about bringing her children to the ice show, hoping it would somehow brighten their lives. Today marked an anniversary of sorts—four years to the day since Robert had died. Four years, and Bobby was still having trouble understanding why his dad had been taken from them. It was good to see the children behaving normally, fussing at one another on a day that, otherwise, could have been a sad one for all of them.

She tousled the agitator's hair and gave him a sly wink. "Bobby, leave your sister alone. Watch for the prince, okay?"

The kettledrums rumbled; the music swelled to a loud crescendo, then dropped again as a lone voice sang, "I'll find my love someday—someday when my prince shall come. . . ."

"There! There he is—he's coming!" Carlee turned her daughter's head with one hand and pointed to the far corner of the big arena with the other. "See him, Becca? There! Right where the fog is thickest!"

Becca squealed with delight. "I see him! I see him!"

Out of the fog in a flash of speed and grace, clad in gleaming white satin, skated Prince Charming in all his glory.

"That's him, Bobby! The man I told you about." Carlee excitedly turned to her son, who was sitting on the edge of his seat watching the male skater. "Keep practicing and you'll be able to do a spread-eagle like that." She pinched his arm lightly. "Yours is pretty good already, for an eight-year-old."

As the music slowed to a romantic pace, so did the prince as he performed an audience favorite—a long, graceful spiral.

Suddenly the music stopped, and so did the performer. An aura of anticipation filled the air as the hall became silent and the heavy fog crawled swiftly across the ice, creeping into all four corners, eerily hovering around the feet of the prince as he caught sight of Snow White. He pushed off with one foot and glided slowly toward the sleeping beauty.

"Isn't he gonna kiss her and wake her up?"

Carlee smoothed her daughter's hair and tried to mask her amusement as she viewed eyes watery with concern. "Just wait, Becca! Keep watching."

Deliberately, lovingly, the skater lowered his face to the maiden's pink lips with a gentle, lingering kiss, as a single violin played softly.

Snow White's lashes fluttered. The dwarfs gasped and began chattering to one another. She blinked her eyes, then opened them wide as she sat up and stretched—first one arm and then the other—followed by an exaggerated yawn.

The prince took her dainty hand in his and lifted it to his lips as she lowered her feet to the ice and stood before him. The bright blue bodice of her snug-fitting dress accentuated her small waist as the flowing red skirt fluttered and billowed about her slender hips. The perfectly matched couple began to move to the music—slowly at first, then more rapidly as they danced across the ice, the spotlight following their every twist and turn, ending with the *crème de la crème,* the phenomenal death spiral and a final kiss.

With the clanging of cymbals and the banging of kettledrums, the music ended. The bright lights shut off. The arena was encased in darkness as the crowd burst into thunderous applause. Spotlights exploded forth, penetrating the blackness of the room, moving in erratic zigzag patterns across the ice in a brilliant assortment of colors. But Snow White and Prince Charming were nowhere to be seen.

Becca tugged at her mother's sleeve again.

Carlee smiled at her daughter. "Be patient, Becca." The beams of light moved collectively to the center of the ice and focused there as Snow White skated into the lighted area, lifted one side of her long red skirt, and curtsied. The audience went wild with applause.

Prince Charming skated into the circle of light and bowed low. Again the crowd went wild, cheering, whistling, and clapping as they gave the pair a standing ovation. Then, out of the darkness, six miniature men skated into the light and dropped to their knees around the beautiful couple, enjoying their portion of the well-deserved applause.

Bobby counted aloud, "One, two, three, four, five, six. Someone's missing!"

"It's Dopey!" Becca shouted. "Where's Dopey?"

From a far corner, the little man skated clumsily into the spotlight, clutching a huge bouquet of long-stemmed red roses in his stubby arms. When he lifted them to Snow White, she bent and kissed him on the nose, to everyone's delight.

Dozens of spotlights in every color of the rainbow began

to weave intertwining ovals as the rest of the Ice Fantasy cast skated onto the ice to receive accolades. "Ladies and gentle-men," the voice of the announcer echoed from the loud-speakers as the houselights came on, "thank you for coming, and drive home safely. Good night."

A single hand wound its way out from under the double-wedding-ring quilt and punched the snooze button when the alarm clock jangled. Six A.M. was still dark. Saturday wasn't a school day, so the kids could sleep in, but Carlee had to get up as early today as she did every other day of the week. She fumbled for the snooze button a second time but decided against prolonging the agony and threw back the covers.

She'd barely finished her toast and was working on a glass of juice when she heard the key turn in the lock of the out-side door and a tall, slender woman with salt-and-pepper hair entered the kitchen. " 'Morning, Mother Bennett."

The smiling woman placed a cookie sheet on the table and tugged at the fingers of her glove. " 'Morning, yourself. How was the ice show?" She lifted the linen napkin covering the pan. The aroma of hot, freshly baked cinnamon rolls loaded with caramel and pecans filled the country kitchen. "Can I tempt you with these?"

"Oh, my favorite! Mother Bennett, you spoil us." Carlee grabbed a sticky roll and kissed her mother-in-law. "When did you bake these? It's barely 6:15."

"Last night; reheated them this morning. I knew how hard this week would be for you. I wanted to do something spe-cial, to help you get through it. You'd better get going."

Carlee gulped her juice, wrapped the remainder of her cinnamon roll in a napkin, and wiggled into her heavy jacket. "See you at noon."

Once at the ice rink that she owned jointly with her in-laws, Carlee flipped on the string of lights and slipped into the little snack bar where the electric oil-filled heater waited to be plugged in. She filled the coffeepot, flipped the "on" switch, and pulled her coat close about her neck.

The buzzer on the outside door sounded. A quick look through the peephole revealed four mothers with four children, each child holding a pair of ice skates. Carlee lifted the latch and held the door open as they filed in, one by one.

"Sure hated to get out of bed this morning," one of the mothers admitted as she sniffed the air. "Coffee smells good."

Carlee grinned and gestured toward the perking pot. "It'll be ready in a minute."

"Did you see the ice show at the Kemper?" a yawning mother asked as she plopped onto a stool and leaned her head against the wall. "That Dan Castleberry is a real hunk."

"Skates good, too," another added. "You agree, Carlee?"

She nodded, then turned her attention to the sleepy children, who stood watching like zombies. "It's time for you guys to get those skates on. Your patch is waiting."

"Don't you ever get tired of getting up this early to let people in to skate?" a mother asked as she poured herself a second cup of coffee. "Sometimes I wonder if it's worth it."

Carlee pulled a caramel-covered pecan from her roll and looked thoughtful. "No, not really. Working at this rink makes it possible for me to take good care of my children and be home with them when they need me. I can't complain."

After Robert's death, Carlee had insisted that she carry her share of the load. Her father-in-law couldn't handle it by himself. Their agreed-upon arrangement had worked out perfectly, with Ethel Bennett serving as the willing, available baby-sitter. Carlee was less than three weeks pregnant when Robert died in the plane crash; he never knew about his daughter.

In the little office with its clear view of the rink, Carlee sat and punched the calculator. Father Bennett ran the afternoon and evening skating sessions, but she was the one who tallied and recorded the sessions and filled out the bank deposits, just as Robert had when he was alive.

She watched with amusement as an overweight girl in her midteens struggled with her three-turns as her mother gruffly barked advice from the first row. *Please, Lord, don't let me ever do to that to my children,* she silently prayed.

Praying for her children came easy; she'd learned at an early age to talk to God about anything and everything, even things that would seem foolish to most people. Only one time could she remember praying for or about something and receiving no answer: that had been prayer for her beloved Robert. Without realizing it, she began to sing softly as she worked, "Someday, my prince will come. . . ."

It was five minutes past noon when Carlee slipped quietly through the kitchen door. A pot of homemade vegetable beef stew simmered on the stove. Mother Bennett's sweet voice could be heard as she sat in the rocking chair reading *Snow White and the Seven Dwarfs* to an appreciative four-year-old. The young mother tiptoed into the room and seated herself carefully on the sofa beside Bobby. Mother Bennett looked up, but Becca was too engrossed in the story to notice Carlee.

"And they lived happily ever after. The end!" Mother Bennett announced with a flourish as she closed the book.

Becca kissed her grandmother's cheek before leaping off her lap and into her mother's. Carlee cradled her baby to her breast and said gratefully, "Thanks, Mother Bennett. You're very special."

Her mother-in-law crossed the room and squeezed Carlee's shoulder affectionately. "So are you. Enjoy the soup."

Carlee watched as Ethel pulled on her coat and headed for her own home, only a hundred feet from theirs. Since Robert's death, Ethel had been coming over at 6:15 every morning to care for the children so Carlee could open the rink for the "patchers," as they called them. By now, it was a ritual. Carlee would return home, eat, and then take some of the soup to Father Bennett. He'd eat, kiss her good-bye, and head for the rink in time to open at 1:30. At 4:00, 4:30, and 5:00 o'clock, he would give private lessons, then run home for a bite of supper and be back to the rink by 6:30 to give a group lesson. Then he would open for the evening session at 7:30. But it was Mother Bennett who kept them all going. She worked quietly in the background, caring for the children all morning so Carlee could work and be home with them the rest of the day.

two

When Carlee rolled out of bed Sunday morning at seven, a luxury she enjoyed only once a week, Mother Bennett was sitting in the kitchen sipping freshly brewed coffee. "How long have you been here? Why didn't you wake me?" The younger Mrs. Bennett poured herself a mug of hot coffee and plopped into the oak pressed-back chair.

"Came over early. I didn't mind the wait—I knew you could use the extra sleep. Besides, it's Sunday."

The young woman wearily rose to her feet and pulled on her heavy jacket. "That means I'd better hustle if I'm gonna close out last night's receipts and get the kids ready for Sunday school."

"Want me to go with you, Mama?" Bobby stood there, dressed in jeans and a flannel shirt, his feet covered with the worn cowboy boots he loved so much.

Carlee reached out a hand and grinned at her son. "Sure! I'd love the company."

The rink seemed exceptionally cold when they entered. She set about counting the admissions and preparing the bank deposit. Bobby placed the nickels, dimes, and quarters in the tray, counting them aloud as he deposited each coin. The two were startled by the sound of the buzzer. She checked her watch: 7:45. Maybe one of the skaters forgot what day of the week it was; who else would be buzzing on Sunday?

"I'll get it!" Bobby volunteered as he jumped from the stool and raced toward the door, ready to fling it open.

"No, Bobby! Wait!" his mother cautioned, her hands full

of dollar bills, half-counted. "Don't open the door!"

Bobby climbed onto a chair and peered out the peephole.

"Mom!" he shouted as he leaped from the chair and ran toward his mother, a broad smile dominating his freckled face. "It's Prince Charming! He's at our door!" He grabbed his mother by the arm and dragged her from the stool. "Aren't you going to let him in?"

Carlee drew back. "Bobby; stop! Prince Charming wouldn't be at our door, especially this time of morning. It's Sunday. He's miles from here by now."

Bobby was relentless. "Yes, he is, Mommy. Honest! It's him; I know it is. Come and see!" He released his hold and ran back to the peephole as the buzzer sounded a second time.

Carlee placed the money tray and the loose bills in the drawer and locked it securely, then hurried to the door. Sure enough, there stood Prince Charming, waiting patiently.

"See, Mom? I told you so!" Bobby tugged at the dead bolt on the door as his mother stood gazing out the peephole. "Mom, he's cold! Let him in!"

Carlee took one last look, then opened the door.

"Hi." The handsome skater smiled at the dazzled young mother and her son. "I saw your car parked by the door and hoped someone would be here. Do you rent ice time here at the Ice Palace?"

Bobby yanked at her sleeve. "Mom—say something."

"Yes. No. I mean, yes, we do, but not on Sunday." She felt like a dork as she stood in the doorway, her hair barely combed, her frayed jacket zipped to the neck. She was sure he didn't recognize her, not the way she looked.

The man smiled at Bobby. "Hey, kid, you a skater?"

Bobby returned his smile. "Yep. But not as good as you."

"Oh, you've seen me skate, have you? At the show here in Kansas City this week?" He stuffed his hands deeply into his pockets and shivered.

Carlee blushed and stepped back. "The building is cold, but at least the wind isn't blowing in here."

He strode in and closed and locked the door behind him. She should have been frightened, but after all, she had met him before, if only for a minute. And he *was* Prince Charming; surely Prince Charming would do them no harm.

"Let me introduce myself—officially." He winked at Bobby as he extended a gloved hand. "I'm Dan Castleberry."

Bobby stood straight and tall and reached out his hand to shake the skater's. "Hi, I'm Bobby Bennett. This is my mom."

Dan Castleberry shook the small hand vigorously. "Pleased to meet you, Bobby. What a fine, well-mannered young man you are." Then, looking at the boy's mother, the man did a double take. "You're the woman I met at Wal-Mart!"

Frozen to the spot, she responded with a dull, "Uh-huh," and nodded her head and wished she didn't look so dowdy.

"Well, then, Mrs. Bennett, you may know Kansas City was the last stop on our tour; we've been traveling for two years with this production. I have three weeks off before we begin rehearsals for the new show." He looked at the boy. "I'm here to visit my parents, Bobby. They live in Overland Park. I need to start practicing my new role as the Beast." He laughed, screwed up his face, and crossed his eyes. "I'd like to stay in Kansas City and spend time with my parents. But, I have to find an available rink in this area or I'll have to go on to Florida to begin practice."

Carlee listened intently, trying to keep her mind from wandering to thoughts of him skating so beautifully in that white satin costume.

"So, I'll take any time you have available. And of course, I'll pay whatever the going rate is. I'd like to have at least an hour a day—more if I can get it."

Carlee pursed her lips awkwardly, wishing that, at the least, she'd put on a little lipstick. Well, too late for that!

"Mom. . ." Bobby nudged her side with his elbow.

"I'll—uh—have to ask my father-in-law," she responded weakly, still in shock at seeing the prince. "But I'm sure he'll work something out for you." She pulled Bobby in front of her and wrapped her arms about him, almost as a shield.

"I need to get started as soon as I can. Tomorrow, if possible." He grabbed the boy by the hand. "Hey, Bobby. How about showing me the ice?"

Bobby pulled away from his mom and led the man toward the big double doors. "Sure," he said with youthful enthusiasm.

Carlee hurried to the phone and called Father Bennett. "What do *you* think about this, Carlee? It'll have to be early in the morning—that's the only time an hour or more is available. You'll have to stay there with him. Are you willing to be there by 5:15? That's pretty early."

She grinned and shifted her weight from one foot to the other. "What's the difference?—5:15, 6:15, early is early! And he's willing to pay whatever we ask," she added as she peered through the windows of the double doors and watched her son's mouth moving rapid-fire. How she wished she could hear his conversation with the man.

"It's fine with me," he agreed.

The double doors swung open, and the man and boy came strolling through, laughing and talking like old friends. Sadness welled up in Carlee's heart. How much her son had missed without a father to talk to and be with.

Dan raised his brows. "Well, what's the good word?"

She pushed her hair from her forehead and smiled, first at Bobby, then the skater. "If you can come mornings by 5:15, you'll have a whole hour. Is that acceptable?"

He rubbed his hands together briskly. "Great. And thanks, I appreciate it. I think my folks will, too."

She moved toward the door and unlocked it. "Sorry, but we have to leave or we'll be late for Sunday school."

"Oops, I'm the one who's sorry! Hope I didn't keep you too long." He ruffled up Bobby's hair with his big hand before stepping through the open door. "See ya at 5:15 tomorrow morning!"

Bobby ran to his mom and gave her a bear hug. "Wow! Prince Charming! Wait'll I tell the kids at Sunday school!"

Dan Castleberry sat in his car with the motor running, listening to the radio and thinking of his future. He checked his watch: five o'clock. He'd arrived early, anxious to start practicing his new assignment as the Beast. He drummed his fingertips on the steering wheel in time to the music. What if Mrs. Bennett had forgotten about him? No, not likely. He had a feeling she was more responsible than that. He'd liked the woman immediately, but he had wondered why any man would allow his wife to be out this time of the morning, meeting with a stranger. She had to be married; he'd noticed the wedding band on her left hand. And he'd met her son.

A bread truck pulled into the parking lot and stopped next to his car. The driver waved, placed boxes of buns on the empty rack standing beside the door, and drove off. Headlights splashed across Dan's face as a minivan pulled into the parking lot and parked beside him. The lone occupant, a woman, opened the door and stepped out. He smiled, waved to her, and turned off the engine.

Carlee returned his smile, waved back, and moved to open the door. He followed her in, shut the door, and turned the dead bolt. A sudden chill ran down her spine; she was locked in the building at 5:15 in the morning, alone with a man she barely knew. She moved quickly to turn on the long string of florescent ceiling lights, and the area was instantly flooded with a harsh, glaring brilliance. She could feel his eyes watching her as he stood silently near the door.

"Okay if I go on in and get my skates on?" he asked.

Suddenly she felt ridiculous. This was a business arrangement. He was there to practice—nothing else. "Sure. Of course," she called back over her shoulder and headed toward the snack bar. "You drink coffee? I'll have some ready in a few minutes." But her words were wasted; he'd already disappeared into the rink to lace up his skates.

When the coffee finished dripping, she poured two steaming mugfuls and slipped quietly through the double doors. There he was, etching perfect figure-eights onto the ice.

"Come and take time out for a cup of coffee. It'll help warm you up," she invited as she placed his mug onto the smooth railing that surrounded the ice.

He finished the figures, then glided silently toward her and sipped the coffee. "Umm, good. Thanks." He leaned against the railing and held the warm mug between cold hands. With his skates on, he was nearly a head taller than Carlee, and she had to look up to see his smile.

"I know you don't know much about me, Mrs. Bennett, but I want you to assure you—I *am* trustworthy." He took a big swallow of coffee and grinned at her. "You're perfectly safe with me."

She lowered her gaze to the floor to avoid his eyes. Had he sensed her fear? It wasn't that she was afraid; it was just that she hadn't been this alone with a man since Robert died, and there was something so intimate about meeting a strange man in a deserted ice rink at 5:15 in the morning.

"I know. . .I. . .uh. . .don't mean to keep you. From skating, I mean." She felt herself stumbling over her words.

He took a last swig and gave a slight chuckle. "You're not. I needed the coffee. Thank you," he said warmly.

"I'll go back to the office and give you some privacy," she explained as she pulled her scarf about her neck and began to head toward the doors with the empty mugs.

"I'm used to skating before an audience, remember?" He

did a quick twirl and added, "Honest; I'd like you to stay. Maybe you can help me with this routine."

"Uh. . .sure." She lowered herself into a front-row seat. "What can I do?"

He winked a friendly wink. "I'll let you know."

She tightened the loop on her scarf, buttoned the top button on her jacket, and pulled her gloves onto chilled, stiff fingers, then watched in awe as the professional skater went through an old routine to loosen up. He stopped at the far end of the rink and stood watching her, then skated with strong, quick strokes directly toward her. As he came within a few feet, he quickly turned the edges of his blades into the rink's surface and showered the empty chairs next to her with a blizzard of finely shaved, snowy ice. "*Now* you can help me," he said with a mischievous laugh.

She brushed a few stray ice fragments from her sleeve and returned his smile. "How?"

He pulled an audiotape from his jacket pocket and handed it to her. "Can you put this on for me?"

She crossed the rink, loaded the tape player, and punched "play." The theme song from *Beauty and the Beast* filled the rink and he began to skate. She slipped back into her chair and watched in amazement. From time to time he'd stop, listen to the music, and start again, as though receiving instructions from some unseen source.

The hour was up all too soon, but he quit right on time.

"All right with you if I leave the tape here?"

"Sure," she mumbled as he sat down beside her and began to loosen the laces on his skates.

"How about the skates?"

"Uh, I'll lock them up in the office," she volunteered.

The buzzer sounded on the outside door. The first group of regulars were ready to begin their patch session. Dan allowed the skaters to enter before exiting through the door, then closed it behind him.

"Who was *that?*" one of the mothers asked as she riveted her eyes on the closed door.

"Prince Charming," Carlee said coyly with a wink, leaving the stranger's true identity to their imaginations.

three

He was sitting on the fender of his car when she drove into the parking lot. There were things he wanted to know about Carlee Bennett—like, where was her husband? Were they divorced? He caught up with her, took the key from her hand, and turned it in the lock.

"Been waiting long?" she asked breathlessly.

"Nope. Just arrived." He pushed open the door and stood back to allow her to enter, then locked the door behind them with a sheepish grin. "How can you look this great so early in the morning?"

She was both surprised and pleased by his question. She tucked a lock of hair behind one ear and smiled shyly. "Considering all the beautiful women you skate with, I must seem like plain Jane. But thanks anyway."

He stepped in front of her, spread his arms, and blocked her way. "I don't give compliments unless I mean them."

Carlee flashed an embarrassed smile and gave his arm a friendly pat. "Turn on the lights. I'll get your skates."

She filled the coffeepot and stood waiting for the water to filter through. By the time the last drop had fallen into the glass pot, he was already on the ice, etching perfect eights with his skate blades. When he looked her way, she lifted his mug to let him know it was ready and waiting.

This time he skated over and sat down on the seat beside her, their elbows touching. "Tell me about yourself, Mrs. Bennett. Does your husband skate?" He sipped the hot coffee nonchalantly, as though merely making conversation.

"Please; call me Carlee," she corrected through chattering

teeth as she turned to face him, her bright eyes barely peeping over the upturned collar.

He fingered his empty cup. "Only if you'll call me Dan."

"Dan," she repeated slowly. "Were you named after your father?"

"No. How about Bobby—was he named after *his* dad?"

Carlee smiled as she thought of Robert. "Yes, he was." She pressed back a tear but it ran slowly down her cheek.

Dan pulled the paper napkin from around his mug and gently blotted the tear from her face.

"Sorry," she whispered through a watery smile. "It's been four years; you'd think I'd have gotten beyond doing this—"

"He left you when Bobby was four?"

"No! He died!" Carlee protested as she turned quickly toward him and lifted moist eyes to meet his. "Robert would never leave us; he loved us. We had a perfect marriage."

Looking as though he felt a little foolish, Dan continued asking questions. "How did he die?"

"Plane crash," she answered with a slight sniffle.

He fingered the handle on his cup. "Oh. Sorry."

The two sat quietly, sipping their coffee.

"You probably think I'm silly to be so emotional after four years." She forced a smile. "I miss him so much."

"I think it's wonderful. If anything ever happened to me, I'd want my wife to feel just like you do," he confessed.

She wiped away another tear, but continued to smile. "You're married, Dan? To one of those gorgeous women in the show?"

He laughed, a good belly laugh. "No way! You should see 'em without their makeup!"

"Have you ever considered marriage?" she asked, amazed at herself for prying into a stranger's personal life.

"Marriage? No! I'm not about to ruin my life."

His comment surprised her. "That's pretty cynical."

"Not really. I've seen too many marital disasters. The last thing I want to do is get saddled with a wife and kids. No alimony and child support for *this* guy."

His statement threw her off balance and offended her. He made marriage sound like a cataclysm, something to be avoided at all costs. That was certainly not the way she saw it.

"But not all marriages are like that!" she defended as she turned down the collar on her coat.

"Name one that isn't," he scoffed.

"Mine, for one. Mine and Robert's."

"Oh, really? Are you trying to tell me you'd never considered cheating on your husband? Not even once?"

A deep scowl crossed her face and lingered there, all traces of any previous smile gone. "No! Never! I would never do that!"

He scanned her face, then frowned and said softly, "Next, I suppose you're going to tell me you were a virgin on your wedding day."

The heat rose in her cheeks at his comment. So personal. So blunt. "Yes, that is exactly what I'm telling you, Mr. Castleberry. I was a virgin, and so was Robert."

"And you believed him? That he hadn't—that there hadn't been other women before you? None of my acquaintances can truthfully make that claim. Most guys wear their conquests like a badge of victory. You'd be surprised how many guys brag about it."

This conversation infuriated her. "Does that include you?" she asked with fire in her eyes. She wanted to slap him for even suggesting there may have been improprieties in her life. Or Robert's. She clenched her fists angrily and answered his question before he could answer hers. "You needn't answer. But yes, I did believe him. We both were raised to have high standards, something that you apparently don't understand. I feel sorry for you, Dan Castleberry. To never love someone enough to trust them, to commit your life to them, to experience true oneness with your mate. Well, that's missing out one of God's biggest blessings in life."

She could feel her heart pounding; rarely did anyone stir up her emotions like this. "Don't underestimate marriage, Dan. Granted, being married to the wrong person could be miserable. But if you're married to the one God intended for you—"

"Like Robert?"

She forced a slight smile. "Yes. Like Robert. Then marriage can be beautiful, especially if it's blessed with children." There, she'd said enough. Subject closed!

They sat silently as he continued to finger the handle on his coffee mug and she stared at the ceiling. They'd been having such good, light conversation. It had turned so quickly.

She crossed her arms over her chest, breathed deeply, and tried to get control of her anger. How could he possibly understand her position on marriage? On life? Why should he? Her anger turned to pity. Without God's leading, life was merely living, years passing by with no true purpose.

Dan broke the heavy silence. "Hey, look. I'm sorry. I guess I come from a different world than yours. I didn't mean to come off so strongly. Guess I'm pretty opinionated." He shifted nervously in the chair. "And as to your question," he explained with a look of sincerity that said *I'm telling the truth,* he went on, "No, that did *not* include me. I have no conquests to boast about, no badges of victory." He lowered his chin and mumbled softly, so softly she wasn't sure she'd heard him right. "Not since. . ." But he didn't finish.

She allowed a slight smile to surface. "I need to apologize now. I have strong opinions, too. It's just that these things are important to me and close to my heart since I'm a Christian."

His hand reached awkwardly toward hers, and she felt the warmth of his fingers grasping hers as he gave them an apologetic pat. "You have nothing to apologize for. I'm sorry for my behavior, and I hope you'll forgive me."

He did come from a different world. Why should she expect him to share her perspective on marriage and fidelity? She felt sorry for him. He appeared to have so much, yet had so little. Disagreeing with Dan wasn't going to accomplish anything, and she wanted to be a testimony to him.

"I know you don't like kids, Dan, but Bobby thinks you're wonderful. He asked me if he was going to get to see you again before you leave."

"Hey," he returned defensively, "I like kids! I just don't want any of my own. Sure, I'd like to see him. Especially since he's a skater." He bent over and tightened the laces on his skate. "Tell me when he'll be here and I'll make a point to come by. Maybe I can give him a few pointers."

Her eyes brightened at the thought. "Oh, he'd love that! I could bring him by Wednesday afternoon after school—say about four o'clock? One of the patchers won't be in this week. Bobby could skate on her area. Would that work for you?"

"Wednesday it is!" he confirmed as he jumped over the railing and onto the ice. "Now, if you'll put that tape on the machine, I've got practicing to do."

&

Bobby ran to tell the neighbor kids when he heard that Dan wanted to watch him skate.

"Doesn't he want to watch *me* skate, Mama?" Becca asked as she combed the long, tangled hair on her Barbie doll.

Carlee lifted the little girl and gave her a big hug. "Of course he wants to watch you skate, honey."

"Mama, does he wear his Prince Charming suit when he skates at our rink?" the tiny girl asked as she struggled to extricate the brush from the doll's hair.

Carlee tried to restrain a laugh. "No, sweetie. Just jeans and a plaid shirt kinda like Bobby wears."

&a.

When Mother Bennett arrived Wednesday morning, Carlee was fully dressed and sipping coffee in the kitchen.

"You're up early." Ethel handed her daughter-in-law a brown paper bag, its top folded over like a lunch sack.

"What's this?"

Mother Bennett patted her hand and said with a curious smile, "I thought it'd be nice if you and Mr. Castleberry had some homemade chocolate chip cookies for your coffee break."

&a.

Dan was leaning against the door when Carlee arrived at the rink. His spirits had lightened since he'd thought over their conversation about Robert. The last thing he was interested in was a young widow with a son, but, although he was sorry for her loss, he was relieved to find there was no ex-spouse or deadbeat dad in her life. Losing a husband that way must have been tough on her. She seemed to have weathered it well.

"You're early," she chastised cheerily as she handed him the key and glanced at her watch.

"You're pretty," he replied as he unlocked the door and pushed it open with his shoulder.

She quickly entered and headed toward the coffeepot with her sack of goodies. "Flatterer."

"What's this?" He leaned over the counter and picked up the brown bag. "Goodies for our break time?"

She slapped his hand and grabbed the sack. "You'll find out soon enough. Now, go!"

He saluted and headed for her office to get his skates.

The coffee seemed to take longer than usual to perk. By the time she carried the mugs into the rink, he had finished his school figures and was skating in a long, easy-flowing circular pattern. When he noticed her, he skated over and showered the area with the customary cascade of snowy ice, and as usual, she laughed and brushed it from her sleeve.

"You don't have to serve me refreshments every morning, you know." He took the hot mug of coffee and sniffed its pleasant aroma. "Umm. Just what I needed."

"Oh?" she teased as she dangled and swung the brown bag before his eyes, just out of his reach. "Look what I've got!"

"Give me that," he ordered with a twinkle in his eye as he lunged at the elusive bag. His cheek brushed hers in the process, and he backed off quickly, embarrassed.

She pretended it hadn't happened, opened the bag, and showed him the six giant chocolate chip cookies. "Mother Bennett baked these for us. Go on—take one. Don't be shy."

He pulled a cookie from the bag, took a big bite, and rubbed his tummy with his palm. "Thank Mother Bennett for me; these are great! Homemade, huh?"

She reached into the bag, selected a cookie for herself, and munched on it pensively. "Dan, you said you wanted to stay in the Kansas City area so you could spend time with your parents. Are you close to them?"

He took another bite and looked off into space with a melancholy look. "Not very. Traveling so much makes it impossible to see them very often. I call at least twice a week, but it's not the same as being with them."

She offered the bag and he took a second cookie.

"You're close to your in-laws?" he asked. "And they take good care of your son while you're working here?"

"And Becca."

Dan looked puzzled. "Becca? Who's Becca?"

"My four-year-old daughter, Rebecca. Bobby's little sister. The delight of my life!" Hadn't she mentioned Becca? Dan raised his eyebrows in surprise, then frowned thoughtfully. "If Becca is four and Robert died four years ago, that means she was just a little baby when he died. She probably doesn't even remember her dad."

Carlee dipped her head and blinked hard. "Worse than that; he didn't even know about her. She was born eight months after his death. Neither of us knew I was pregnant at the time. Those were the hardest eight months of my life." She stood awkwardly and stretched as mixed emotions surged through her chilled body. "My in-laws live next door. Grandma comes over every morning. I come in here, work till noon, then go home. Want the rest of the schedule?"

He nodded.

She brushed the crumbs from her jacket and continued. "She goes home and fixes lunch for Father Bennett. He comes to the rink and works the rest of the day." She took a deep breath and let it out slowly, with a grin. "Then I come back the next morning and the cycle begins all over again. It's a good, workable schedule for all of us, and this way, we can keep the business in the family. They want me to be with the children as much as possible, and they're willing to do whatever is necessary to help make it happen." She shoved the bag toward him once more. "Sounds boring, doesn't it?"

He shook his head and held up a hand. "No more for me; I've got skating to do!" He stood, grabbed the bag from her hands, and folded its top. "But I'll eat the rest of them when I finish. Keep 'em for me, okay? And don't forget to thank Grandma!"

Some of the patchers arrived earlier than usual; there was only time to shout a brief good-bye and a quick reminder that Bobby would be watching for him around four o'clock. Dan nodded and assured her he'd be there as he shut the door behind him.

The four mothers turned to watch him go, still not used to seeing Prince Charming in the Ice Palace.

four

Gray clouds moved across the Kansas City sky as Dan Castleberry stared at the clock in the dashboard of his rented car; it was 3:30, and he was early. He'd never skated with an eight-year-old before. Could the little boy really skate? If Dan had a son, that's the way it'd be—he'd have skates on the kid as soon as he took his first steps.

Dan laughed aloud, a real belly laugh. A son? His son? Like he'd told Carlee, he'd never even considered marriage, let alone children! When you travel from city to city and country to country, spending only a week at a time in any one place, marriage isn't in your vocabulary. No, as long as he was skating professionally, marriage was out of the question. He'd have plenty of time for that later, when and if the idea of marriage ever appealed to him. But would he ever meet a woman he could trust? One he'd want to marry? One who wouldn't marry him, then take him to the cleaners for alimony?

The conversation he'd had with Carlee about her marriage to Robert replayed in his mind. He'd like a woman to be pure, to have kept herself for him only, like Carlee had for Robert, but he was nearly twenty-nine. Was there any woman his age who had remained pure? Not likely! He slumped in the seat, leaned back against the headrest, and closed his eyes as he mentally began to skate through his new routine.

≈

"Mom, do you think he'll remember to come?" Bobby asked from the backseat as they whizzed through traffic.

Carlee winked at her son in the rearview mirror. "Of course he'll remember, Bobby. That's the last thing he said

29

this morning, 'See you at four o'clock!' He'll be there."

And sure enough, there was Dan's rental car, parked next to the building by the front door. Apparently hearing the sound of their engine, he straightened up and waved.

"Dan, I'm so sorry we're late," she called to him as she unbuckled Becca's seat belt. "Heavy traffic."

He locked his car and strolled over to where they were parked, never taking his eyes off the beautiful little girl.

"So, this must be Becca." He saw she was the image of her mother with soft, reddish-brown hair and incredibly blue eyes.

Becca smiled and wrapped her arm around her mother's leg as she shyly twisted a lock of her hair.

"This is Mr. Castleberry, Becca, the nice man you watched in the ice show. Remember? Prince Charming." She tugged at Becca's arm and tried to break free of her daughter's grasp. "Sorry, Dan. Normally she's not this shy. I think she's intimidated at meeting Prince Charming. We all are," she confessed reluctantly as she stroked Becca's hair.

"Well, it's nice to meet you, Becca. I hope we can be friends. I've never been friends with a four-year-old before." His warm smile might have been intended for the little girl, but it melted a proud mother's heart.

Carlee watched as Dan took Bobby's hand in his, opened the door, and disappeared into the rink.

By the time Dan and Bobby reached the ice, Carlee and Becca were already seated, waiting. Bobby had warned his mother that he didn't want her hovering over him during his time with Dan, so she'd chosen two seats that were several rows up and off to one side, where she and Becca wouldn't be quite so conspicuous.

Bobby stepped onto the ice first as Dan stood by the railing, watching. The patch didn't give Bobby much room to work but he gave it his all. Carlee didn't watch her son. She watched Dan's jaw drop in amazement as he moved onto the ice beside Bobby and the two began to talk.

"That's the Prince Charming we've heard so much about?"

The young mother turned toward the voice with a smile as an athletic-looking man in his early fifties dropped into the seat beside her and pulled Becca onto his lap. Becca squealed with delight and pulled his cap down over his eyes.

"Hi, Father Bennett," Carlee said, nodding her head. "Yep, that's him. I think he's impressed with Bobby's skating."

He pushed his hat from his eyes and tickled his little granddaughter as she giggled and pulled away from his hold. "The kid's a natural; I've taught him everything he knows."

The threesome observed quietly as the professional ice skater worked with Bobby on his school figures, then they hurried toward the end of the rink when the two skaters left the ice. By the time they reached them, Dan and Bobby were already in their street shoes, laughing and wiping ice off their blades with an old towel from Bobby's bag.

Bobby smiled confidently at his mother and grandfather. "Hey, Mom, Mr. Castleberry said he'd teach me some more stuff before he leaves."

Carlee touched her son lightly on his slim shoulder. "Bobby, don't you think it would be nice if you introduced your teacher to your grandfather?"

Bobby took Father Bennett's hand in his. "Oh, yeah. Sorry. Grandpa, this is Mr. Castleberry. Mr. Castleberry, this is my grandpa."

Short and sweet, just like a boy, she thought.

Dan Castleberry extended his hand with a broad smile. "Pleased to meet you, sir. I've heard many nice things about you and Mrs. Bennett—from Carlee and Bobby."

The older man accepted his hand and gripped it firmly. "Nice to meet you. But please, call me Jim."

Dan smiled. "Only if you'll all call me Dan, and that includes you, Bobby." He tousled Bobby's hair. "And you, too, Becca. Will you call me Dan?"

Becca twisted in her grandfather's arms and nodded her head, then leaned forward until her forehead touched Dan's and rested there. "Dan," she said with a giggle.

He looked pleased, his smile bright and warm.

"You in a hurry, Dan?" Jim Bennett asked as he lowered Becca to the floor.

"No, sir. Why?" He shifted his skate bag to his shoulder and lifted his brows.

"Got a few things I'd like to show ya," Jim answered with a friendly wink as he took Dan's arm and led him away.

Carlee watched them go, then called out after them, "Thanks, Dan. See you in the morning."

Dan spun back to answer. "You bet. I'll be there."

⠻

Jim Bennett led Dan Castleberry to his private office down a long hall, just beyond the skate room. "Oh!" said Dan appreciatively when Jim flipped on the lights.

The room was filled with rows of shelves supporting trophies in all sizes, colors, and shapes, each inscribed with the name Jim Bennett. The walls were covered with photos, most in color, a few in black and white. Many of them featured a man skating, spinning, performing jumps, spread-eagles, or spirals. The remainder pictured the same man accepting awards and shaking hands with dignitaries. The featured man was the same in each photo—Jim Bennett!

Dan was impressed. He had no idea that the Jim Bennett who owned and operated the Ice Palace was the same Jim Bennett he'd heard about all his years in the skating world.

"Why didn't Carlee tell me?"

Jim Bennett rubbed his chin. "Guess because she doesn't know a lot about me. Seems like I'm bragging or something. I don't talk about my past much. I quit skating professionally the year Ethel and I got married."

"But, why?" Dan inquired with a puzzled look. "You were at the peak of your profession! Why'd you leave it?"

Jim smiled a secretive little smile. "Love, son. Love."

"Mrs. Bennett?"

"Yep. Couldn't expect her to follow me all over the world. We wanted to settle down and raise a family. So I quit, bought this rink; been here over twenty-five years now."

Dan watched Jim as he talked. It was obvious he'd made the right decision—for him.

"What kind of goals have you set for yourself, Dan?"

Dan leaned forward and looked at the man who'd blazed the professional trail before his time. "You're living it, sir! I want to own my own rink, maybe a couple of rinks. I'd like to train young skaters, maybe even steer some of them toward the Olympics." He leaned back with a modest grin. "I even have a name for my rink."

"Oh?" Jim moved to stand beside his guest. "What?"

Dan straightened in the chair, excited to share his dreams with someone who understood. "Ice Castle!"

Jim grinned as he rubbed the five o'clock shadow forming on his ruddy chin. "Good name! Catchy and appropriate. Owning your own rink is an awesome responsibility, but there's nothing like it." He raked his fingers through his hair thoughtfully. "Umm. Ice Castle. I do like that name."

Dan folded his arms across his chest and sat gazing around the room. Jim Bennett, ice skater extraordinaire, the owner and pro of the Ice Palace. It was too much to comprehend.

"You married, Dan?" His unexpected question came like a thunderbolt out of the blue, startling the young man.

It was a simple question, yet the skater felt uncomfortable answering it, and paused. "No, sir."

Jim seated himself in the straight-backed chair behind the cluttered desk, leaned back, and locked his hands behind his head. "Hate to tell you this, son, but you've been missing the greatest thing God ever arranged for man. A good-looking guy like you should have his pick of women. Is it that you haven't found the right one yet?"

Dan pondered the question. "I'm not sure. I've always thought of marriage as an anchor around your neck—being tied to one person, stripped of your freedom. Now I don't know, especially after a conversation I had with Carlee."

"You mean about Robert?"

"Yes, sir. Robert and their marriage. She made it sound like a good marriage was the ultimate goal in life. Talked like God had planned for them to be together."

Jim let out a long sigh. "And you don't believe her?"

"I honestly think *she* believes it, but could that be? Do you think God really cares about such things?"

Jim templed his fingertips thoughtfully. "Yes, Dan, I do. He's told us in His Word that He's concerned about even the littlest things in our lives." He smiled at Dan across the cluttered desk. "I even think He sent you into our lives."

≥≈

Dan Castleberry stayed at the rink much longer than he'd intended, watching and listening as Jim Bennett gave private lessons. He'd stumbled into a world he hadn't realized existed. In Kansas City, the home of his parents, of all places! He'd expected these three weeks to be routine and dull and that he'd be anxious to get back to join the rest of the cast and rehearsals. Now, the time was passing all too quickly.

≥≈

Carlee and the children had supper at the Bennetts' home that evening. With Jim Bennett, Bobby, and Becca talking about Dan Castleberry, Carlee and Ethel barely got in a word.

"I want to meet this young man," Ethel told her daughter-in-law as the two women cleared the table and loaded the dishwasher. "Maybe he could come to dinner on Sunday. Why don't you invite him?"

five

Carlee told Dan about the invitation to Sunday dinner when he took his break from skating. He crossed his legs and leaned back in the bleacher-type chair, sipping his coffee, and without hesitation answered, "Tell your mother-in-law I'd be happy to come."

She was both surprised and happy. It had been months since either Bennett family had invited guests to their home.

"Now I have a favor to ask." He pulled a videotape from his pocket. "This is a rough run-through of the numbers I'll be performing in the new show. I'll be happy to pay you for your time. I need you to watch the tape while I skate, making sure I'm doing everything in the proper sequence. Could you do that for me?"

"Of course I'll do it, Dan," she replied eagerly. "And I'd never allow you to pay me for it."

"Yes!" he shouted as a doubled-up fist shot into the air, much like she'd seen Father Bennett do when something was going his way. "I'll pick up one of those portable TV-VCR units this afternoon."

"Great. I'm happy to help." She had a sudden flash of an idea and spoke before she had a chance to think it through. "Dan, do you have plans for this evening?"

He looked puzzled. "No. Why?"

At once, she felt brazen and ridiculous. "Never mind."

"Oh, no, you don't! You're not getting off that easy. Why did you want to know about my plans for this evening?" He crossed his arms and waited.

"Well," she began slowly, wishing she'd kept her mouth

shut, "I was thinking, if you don't have any plans, maybe you'd like to come over for hot dogs." She really felt foolish inviting Prince Charming for hot dogs.

"I'll be there," he agreed without hesitation. "What time? I'll need the address."

His quick answer caught her off-guard. "Oh, six, seven. . . whatever works for you," she mumbled incoherently.

A sly smile crept across his face. "Good! Hot dogs are my favorite food!"

❧

When Bobby got home from school, he took one look at the immaculate house and asked, "Who's coming?"

She greeted him with a sideways smile. "You're right; someone is coming for supper tonight. Now put your books away."

Bobby's brow furrowed. "Does that mean we aren't gonna have hot dogs? Remember, Mom, Thursday is hot dog night."

Before she could answer, Becca grabbed her brother's hand and blurted out, "I got a secret, Bobby. Wanna hear it? Prince Charming is gonna eat hot dogs with us."

"Mom?" Bobby ran to his mother and threw both arms around her waist. "Really? Is Becca telling the truth?"

"Would you like that, Bobby?"

His eyes sparkled. "Yeah. He's really coming?"

"Yes, he is. Would you like to help me build a nice big fire in the fireplace? We'll roast our hot dogs there."

The look on Bobby's face caused a tightness around his mother's heart. Was she making a mistake by allowing Dan into their lives? He'd be in Kansas City such a short time. She couldn't stand the thought of Bobby becoming attached to this man, only to lose him like he had his father. But that was different; Dan was only a friend, a short-term friend.

❧

Dan Castleberry stepped onto Carlee's front porch right at

six o'clock. She hadn't been specific about the time, and he hoped he wasn't pushing it by showing up so early. He'd been excited about the invitation all day, ever since he'd left Carlee at the rink nearly twelve hours earlier. He'd even stopped at the florist on the way to their house and picked out a colorful bunch of flowers. He couldn't remember the last time he'd bought flowers for a woman, other than his mother, and usually he wired those.

No more angry words had passed between Dan and Carlee since that early morning at the rink when they'd discussed her virginity. Although the subject had never come up again, it hung heavily between them like an unseen veil. He hoped she'd think of the flowers as a peace offering, but he'd never suggest it to her. Her words had etched themselves indelibly on his being. He'd never forget them.

≈

Carlee checked the house one final time, with inquisitive little Becca at her heels. Everything was in its place. The porch! She hadn't swept the front porch! "Bobby," she ordered as she straightened the coffee table's magazines for the third time, "bring me the broom."

He did as he was told. She smiled at her son, grabbed the broom, and rushed out the door, only to find her expected guest standing on the porch, one hand reaching for the door-bell, the other holding a bouquet of flowers. The startled look that crossed her face was quickly replaced with a broad smile. "Sorry; you surprised me."

He extended the flowers awkwardly. "For you," he said with a smile that reminded her of the way Bobby smiled when he wanted to gain favor. The flowers remained suspended in midair; the intended recipient not quite sure what to do about them.

"Wanna trade?" Dan reached his free hand toward the broom handle, which she was holding onto for support.

"I. . .uh. . .was going to sweep the porch before you came. You know. . .leaves. Leaves have blown. . .up here." She knew she sounded like a bumbling idiot. What was wrong with her?

"You didn't have to do that for me. I really don't mind stepping over a few leaves," he teased.

The blush returned. It seemed to appear often since Dan Castleberry had skated into her life.

"Here. You take the flowers. I'll take the broom and sweep the porch for my supper. Fair trade?"

She relinquished the broom handle and accepted the bouquet. "Thanks—for the flowers. And, sure, sweep if you want." She added, "But, it's really not necessary. Honest!"

Carlee and the children stood in the doorway and watched as he deftly swished the broom to and fro across the concrete porch. The flowers smelled sweet as she held them to her face and rubbed the velvety softness of their petals across her lips. No one had brought her flowers since Robert had died.

"There." He leaned the broom against the brick wall. "All finished! That better pass inspection, Mrs. Bennett; I'm hungry for those hot dogs."

She hadn't noticed, until now, how deep his dimples were. And she liked them. They fit him and his personality.

He followed her and the children into the house, then looked around, taking in everything in the living room. "It's just like I thought it would be. Cozy, cheerful, and warm."

Bobby tugged at his hand. "Come on, Dan. Mama doesn't let us play in this room."

Dan pointed an accusing finger at Carlee. "That so, Mama? You won't let us play in this room? Why not?"

" 'Cause we're messy," Becca volunteered as she pulled a naked Barbie doll out from under the edge of the chintz sofa.

Dan laughed as he lowered himself onto one knee and checked out Becca's unclothed Barbie. "Okay, now that you children have thoroughly embarrassed your mother, how about showing me your rooms?"

He swept Becca up in his arms and placed her on his broad shoulders as the little girl squealed with glee and hollered, "Whee!"

Dan turned to the young boy who was watching his sister with rapt attention. "Lead the way, Bobby."

Bobby looked to his mother for approval, then ran toward his room, followed by Dan with Becca wiggling on his shoulders and Carlee following close behind in a haze of emotions.

After the tour of all the rooms in the house, including the basement, which Carlee hadn't cleaned, their guest plopped himself down in the middle of the family room. He pulled Bobby down with him, playfully pinning the boy to the floor.

"Help me, Becca," Bobby called to his little sister as he struggled to get free.

A giddy Becca rushed toward the dueling duo and threw herself into their midst. Dan pulled her into the fracas as Becca's and Bobby's laughter filled the room and Carlee looked on, her heart bursting with emotion as she viewed the scene. It was difficult to hold back the tears of joy she was experiencing. But, she knew she had no choice. None of them would have understood, and at this point, neither did she.

"Dan, wanna see my baseballs? They're in my closet," Bobby asked when he was too tired to wrestle anymore and needed a way to quit and still save face.

Dan looked pleased. "Sure. Can Becca come too? Is she allowed in your territory?" he asked as he once again hoisted the little girl to his shoulders.

Bobby grinned impishly. "Okay. Just this one time."

Dan lifted his face toward Becca's. "You won't bother any of Bobby's stuff, will you?"

Becca answered by running her hands through Dan's perfectly moussed hair.

"Becca! Stop!" her mother cautioned.

But Dan and the two children didn't hear; they were headed for Bobby's room and the baseballs.

❧

Bobby's room was as neat as a magazine photo. It was obvious his mother's cleaning hand had been there. Dan thought of his own room when he was Bobby's age. His mother had decided a child's room had no place on the second floor with the other perfectly kept bedrooms. She'd hired carpenters to close in the attic area and create a bedroom for her only son when he became old enough to "make a mess," as she called it. And once he'd moved into it, his mother had avoided his room. The cleaning woman knew more about its contents than she did.

"Dan, do you want to see my Bobby Richardson ball?"

Bobby's words brought Dan back to reality. He sat on the boy's bed with Becca still firmly planted on his shoulders as Bobby proudly held the marred baseball in his hands. He took it and examined it carefully. "It's signed!"

"Uh-huh. My dad bought it from a guy 'cause he knew I'd wanna keep it. He told me all about Bobby Richardson."

The skater gave Bobby his full attention as the boy pulled baseball after baseball from a box in his closet. Most of the balls had no monetary value, but they'd been signed by Bobby's T-ball coaches and friends who played ball with Bobby. He was as proud as if they'd been signed by Mickey Mantle himself. Dan handled each one as if it were special.

A wonderful aroma drifted through the house. Bobby placed his hand in Dan's and led him into the family room in time to see Carlee place a tray of steaming hot nachos in the center of the coffee table. "Thought these might tide you over till the fire gets going well enough to roast our hot dogs. And," she added as she offered a box of matches to their guest, "you are appointed chief fire-builder, and Bobby will help you."

Dan lifted Becca from his shoulders and lowered her onto the sofa, then retrieved the badly abused Barbie from the floor and placed it in the little girl's lap. She hugged the doll tightly to her breast. He turned to Carlee with an amused glimmer. "Do all little girls like Barbie dolls?"

Before she could answer, Becca did! "Mama gots more Barbie dolls than me." Turning to her mother, she added, "Mama, show Dan *your* Barbie dolls."

Her mother turned crimson.

"Carlee, is that right?" Dan taunted as he sauntered slowly toward the wide-eyed mother. "Do you really have more Barbie dolls than Becca?"

"Show him, Mama," her daughter insisted as she swung Barbie in wide circles by her long, matted hair.

"Yes, Mama! Show me!" Dan mimicked in a high-pitched falsetto voice as he tilted his head toward the young woman.

Carlee lowered her head shyly, annoyed with Becca for revealing her secret. "Okay, maybe after supper. Right now, you three need to get that fire going."

"Promise? After supper you'll show me your dollies?" Dan kidded as the children giggled.

"After supper, I promise," she said, symbolically crossing her heart. "Now, get that fire going."

While they worked at building the fire, she made several trips to the kitchen, bringing in trays loaded with hot dogs, buns, mustard, relish, catsup, chopped onion, grated cheese, and other goodies. The final tray held a big pot of homemade baked beans. The wonderful scent of bacon-embellished beans in an open pot quickly drew Dan's attention from the full-blown fire he'd prepared for the hot dog cooking. Two exuberant children jumped into his lap. Their mother moved to push them off, saying, "Hey, kids. Leave Dan alone. Come on now! Get off his lap!" She tugged and pulled on Becca, who clung to Dan's neck and wouldn't let go.

Dan gently but firmly took hold of Carlee's wrists and pulled them away from the little girl who clung to him. "Carlee! It's okay. Really. I like it!" He pulled Becca onto his lap and circled his strong arms about her. She instantly stopped struggling and leaned her head against his chest, one small hand twisting at a lock of his hair.

He pulled her closer to him. "You know, Carlee, I never understood why my friends envied me for *not* having any brothers or sisters. My life was pretty lonely. I'd have given anything to have a brother or sister to fight with. I missed so much and I always wondered why my parents never had any more children. Sometimes I thought it was because I was so bad." His slight laugh had a melancholy sound. "Maybe I was too much trouble for them." He rubbed his cheek across the top of Becca's head and sniffed the leftover fragrance of the baby's shampoo. "They don't know what they missed."

Carlee smiled and pulled Bobby onto her lap. The four of them sat quietly gazing into the warm glow of the fire. Dan gently slid his free arm around Carlee's shoulder and found himself envying a dead man.

She stiffened at the touch of his arm, but only for a moment. No man had been that close in four years. How she missed the strength, the security, and the love of a man's protective arm. She relaxed and found herself magnetically drawn to his nearness.

The fire snapped, sparks sizzled, and the room filled with a cozy warmth, but its origin was not the blazing logs; it was generated by the foursome on the sofa. It penetrated their minds, hearts, and bodies as they enjoyed one another's company. Carlee found herself enjoying the closeness a little too much, and it frightened her. She wanted to press herself into Dan's arm, to rest her head on his shoulder, to feel his breath on her hair.

But there was no place in her life for a three-week fling.

And she knew there was no place in Dan's life for a woman with a ready-made family, not that he'd be interested in her. What did she have to offer that he couldn't find in any city, any state? No, she was a nothing in his world. How could she even think there might ever be anything between them?

"Dan!"

"Umm—what?" He'd been caught daydreaming.

"I asked if you'd mind if Bobby prayed before our meal?"

He pulled his arm from behind her and straightened himself on the sofa. "No, go ahead." He lowered his head and closed his eyes. A small boy slipped his hand into Dan's as a tiny hand pushed its way into his other hand. He sneaked a peek and found the children and their mother's heads bowed low as Bobby began to pray.

"Dear Lord, we thank You for this food our mama made. We thank You for Dan being here to eat with us. In Jesus' name, amen."

When Bobby finished praying, Carlee pulled three hot dog holders from a long box and handed one to Bobby, one to Dan, and kept one for herself.

"Where's mine?" Becca asked, her lower lip curling downward.

Dan jumped in. "Oh, Becca. I wanted to cook yours with mine. Please? Won't you let me?"

Becca's disappointment disappeared, and she lifted two arms and encircled them about Dan's neck. "I want my hot dog cooked with yours," she told him with a winning smile that would melt a snowman.

"Mama, I'll cook yours with mine," Bobby volunteered with authority as he poked two hot dogs onto the long spike.

"Good idea," Dan agreed as he slid his free arm around Bobby's shoulder and gave him a wink. "We men will cook the hot dogs; you ladies prepare the buns. Right, Bobby?"

"Right," Bobby replied in a voice much lower than his

usual one. She was surprised to see the young boy mimicking their guest. Her baby boy was growing up.

The hot dogs vanished quickly as the foursome laughed their way through supper. Carlee was amazed at the amount of food her children consumed and concluded it must be due to the joyful atmosphere created by Dan's presence.

"Anyone for dessert?" she asked after the hot dog mess had been banished to the kitchen. "Fresh apple pie loaded with cinnamon and topped with scoops of French vanilla ice cream?"

Dan, Becca, and Bobby all shouted "Yes!" at once.

When it was served, Dan took one bite and frowned.

"What's wrong? Isn't the pie okay?" He'd been so complimentary about her cooking so far; what could be wrong?

He took another bite and closed his eyes. "Ummmm."

"What?" She couldn't imagine what was wrong; the pie tasted fine to her.

His eyes opened slowly, as if he were in deep thought. "I was trying to remember if I'd ever eaten any pie that was better than this pie. And you know what? I haven't!"

A pink flush rose across her face as Carlee smiled.

"This is fantastic," he added as he took another bite. "Did you really bake this, Carlee? From scratch? You're sure it's not from Perkins?"

She was both speechless and flattered by his compliment.

"Mama made the pie. I saw her," Becca said with her mouth full of ice cream.

"Becca," her mother corrected as she applied a napkin to her daughter's delicate face. "How many times have I told you not to talk with your mouth full?"

The little girl swallowed hard and pointed a finger at Dan. "He talked with his mouth full, too. I saw him."

Now it was Dan's turn to blush. "Caught me!"

After supper, Carlee settled the children in front of the TV to watch a new Odyssey videotape that had come in the afternoon mail. Dan watched as she moved about the room tidying up and rearranging pillows. When he caught her attention, he motioned for her to join him on the couch by patting the cushion next to him. The four of them watched and laughed together as the cartoon characters, Dylan and his friends, performed their antics.

"Bedtime!" Carlee announced when the tape ended.

"Aw, Mama, do we have to?" She'd expected rebellion; they'd been having such a good time with Dan.

"Tell you what," Dan proposed as he pulled them both onto his lap. "If it's okay with your mom, after you get ready for bed, I'll tell you a story."

Two children hurried off to don their pajamas as their bewildered mother looked on.

"Hope that's okay with you," Dan apologized.

A grateful smile curled across her lips. "I wouldn't have it any other way."

Two pajama-clad children leaped into Dan's lap and struggled to see who could hug him the tightest as Dan buried his face in first one neck and then the other, giggling and laughing along with them.

"Which book do you want?" Carlee asked as she scanned the shelves that contained the vast assortment of children's books reserved for bedtime reading. "We have quite a selection."

His gray eyes twinkled. "Don't need one; thank you."

His answer surprised her. He'd promised them a bedtime story. Was he going to renege and disappoint them after such a lovely evening?

"Okay, you guys. Settle down. Time for our story." His voice was gentle yet firm as he opened his arms to them.

Two wiry children stopped their wiggling and seated themselves, Bobby on one thigh, Becca on the other. His long arms encircled them, holding them securely. "You have to promise that as soon as the story is finished, you'll go to bed without a word. Okay?"

Two heads nodded in agreement.

"Now, what shall it be, 'Little Red Riding Hood'?"

"Yes!" Becca clapped her little hands as she wiggled on Dan's lap. "I love 'Little Red Riding Hood.' Will you tell us about the wolf, Dan?"

Dan looked at Bobby. " 'Red Riding Hood' okay, fella?"

Bobby grinned. "Yeah. Becca likes it. It's okay."

Dan kissed each child atop the head and began his story. "There once was a beautiful little girl with dark, flowing hair. . ."

The children sat motionless as Dan told the story of the little girl, her grandmother, and the wolf. He included parts of the story Carlee had never heard before, and she found herself as enthralled as the children. When the story ended, Dan again kissed each child on the top of the head, then lifted them both in his arms and carried them to their rooms. Carlee followed silently, not wanting to break the spell.

Becca was the first to be placed in bed. As Dan gently lay her on the Barbie sheets and covered her with the bright pink comforter, she pulled his face down to hers and gave him a forceful kiss on his lips and hugged him tightly. He hugged her back and whispered, "Good night, Becca."

"We didn't pray," the little girl protested.

Dan looked uneasy.

"If you'll put Bobby to bed, I'll pray with Becca," Carlee volunteered quickly, coming to his rescue.

"You got it," he replied as he hurried off with Bobby in his arms, apparently grateful for the reprieve.

Becca drifted off to sleep, exhausted and happy, almost as soon as she said "Amen." Carlee moved to the family room and settled herself in the corner of the couch, her knees drawn up beneath her chin. When Dan joined her, he was smiling.

"What?" His smile intrigued her.

"What what?" he said as he sat down close beside her, crowding her into the corner a bit.

"You were smiling; I wondered why. That's all."

He locked his hands behind his head and rested them against the sofa's soft back. "Didn't realize I was smiling. Guess it was just a smile of contentment. I never had an evening like this when I was growing up. Your kids are lucky."

They sat gazing into the fire as the flames furled and twirled and popped and crackled, spitting sparks wildly against the screen.

"It's hedge," Carlee said matter-of-factly.

"Hedge?" he repeated.

"Hedge pop and crackles like that then spits sparks everywhere, but I like it." She gazed into the fire, enjoying the erratic behavior of the burning hedge wood. Eventually, she lifted her eyes to meet his quizzically. "I have a question. How did you know the story of 'Little Red Riding Hood'? Tonight I heard parts of that story I've never heard before. I was impressed. So were the children."

He winced. "It was okay? They weren't disappointed?"

She touched the tip of his nose with her fingertip. "You told it so well, I've decided I'll never tell it again. I could never do it the way you did."

He let out a sigh. "Okay, I'll let you in on my secret. I've never read 'Little Red Riding Hood' and my mother never read storybooks to me when I was a kid."

"But—how? How did you tell it like that?"

He angled his head toward hers and confessed, "I skated the part of the wolf!"

Apparently, he realized she was laughing at his method of storytelling, not at him, and joined in her laughter.

Dan skating as the wolf conjured up hysterical images. He slid his arm across the sofa back and squeezed her shoulder. "I've had a great evening, but we both have to get up early.

I'd better be going."

    She rose to her feet to walk him to the door. Although she found herself wanting to ask him to stay longer, she resisted the temptation and thanked him for the flowers, now nestled in a crystal vase in the center of the coffee table. As the door closed behind him, she leaned against it and sighed deeply. What a wonderful day this had been!

six

Dan Castleberry climbed in behind the steering wheel and turned the key in the ignition. The engine roared in response. He shoved the gearshift into reverse, but kept his foot on the brake. He wanted one last look at the house—no, at the *home*—rising before him. The laughter had been contagious, and he found himself smiling smugly, as if he had been privy to an episode of love that only a few people could identify with. After this evening, he was anxious to dine at Jim Bennett's home on Sunday and meet Ethel Bennett. Yes, the Bennett family was a unique group of people. To think that there could be that kind of love between a young widow and her in-laws astounded him. So did such love between a mother and her children.

He'd never met another woman like Carlee. There was something so sweet about her—so pure. Just being with her gave him a feeling he'd never known before. How lucky Robert Bennett had been, to have a warm, caring woman like Carlee, who loved him so completely. He hoped someday he could experience that kind of love in his own life.

❧

Carlee hummed as she drove toward the Ice Palace Friday morning. She hated to admit it, even to herself, but she was anxious to see Dan again. They may not see eye-to-eye on marriage and commitment, but he had become a good friend to her and the children. Marriage was the furthermost thing on her mind, too. She'd never find another man like Robert, but she felt safe with Dan. They understood one another's position; there was no room for a permanent relationship in

49

his life, and she certainly wasn't interested in one either. Even if their relationship were more than a mere friendship, it could never develop into anything more than a mild flirtation, and that would end when he left Kansas City.

Her heart skipped a beat despite her thoughts, for there he was, leaning against the building as her headlights scanned the parking lot after she turned off the street. By the time she reached him, he was balancing the big tray of buns on one hand above his head and waiting for her to open the door.

"Oh, so now you're the bread man, huh?" she cajoled as she turned the key and shoved open the door.

"Yes, ma'am," he responded. He headed for the snack bar as she switched on the string of harsh overhead lights.

"I had a great time last night," he whispered into her hair as he passed her on his way back out the door.

"Hey, where are you going?" she called after him.

"To get the VCR! You promised to help me. You haven't changed your mind, I hope."

He inserted the videotape as he lowered the VCR onto the counter and plugged in the machine. "I thought we could run through it once—in here, while we drink our coffee—before I start my practice. That way we can discuss the various moves. Okay with you?"

She nodded her head. "Sure; crank her up. The coffee'll be ready in a minute." She pulled two clean mugs from the shelf while he commandeered two folding chairs. When the coffee was finished, she poured two steaming mugfuls, handed one to Dan, and seated herself beside him as he punched "Play." The familiar theme music sounded from the VCR, and she sat spellbound as she watched Dan skate the entire routine on tape. Even without the costuming and special lighting, it was beautiful. He was extremely talented.

When the routine ended, the music changed and his image appeared on the ice with Valerie Burns by his side. "This is one of the pair numbers we'll be doing in the show. Kinda hard to practice those without a partner," he complained as he fast-forwarded to another of his solo numbers. "You haven't seen this one. I haven't even started practicing it yet."

She didn't understand. If he hadn't started practicing, how had he made the tape?

As if reading her thoughts, he explained. "We made it one small section at a time. The choreographer would show me the move, I'd skate it through a few times, we'd tape it, then stop the tape. By the time we finished and had recorded all the moves, we had the entire routine on tape. That's why it's so jerky—all the stops and starts. But at least it gives me the moves in their proper sequence so I can practice and begin to memorize them in the right order. This is only a start, but it saves time."

She listened intently; it all made sense but sounded difficult. But if this worked, who was she to question it?

They watched until the recorded part ended and the screen filled with snow. While she tidied up the snack bar, he carried the VCR into the ice area and set it up so she could watch from the front row and coach him as he skated.

It worked much better than she'd anticipated. If he'd falter or stop skating, she'd cup her hands to her mouth and shout out the move. When he stopped for his second cup of coffee, he complimented her on her help. "You knew the names of all the moves and called them out like a pro!"

She laughed. "Hey, my father-in-law *is* a pro, remember? I absorbed most of what I know by osmosis."

ॐ

Dan hung around the rink after he finished his session and watched her work before heading home. These days, there was no place he'd rather be than at the rink with Carlee.

When his mother came in from her round of golf, he asked her a strange question. "Where can I buy a doll?"

She lifted manicured fingers to his forehead. "Do you have a temperature, Daniel? I do think you are delirious."

He assured her he was not, but merely wanted to purchase several dolls as gifts for people who had befriended him.

"I think I would try the toy store in the Plaza." She shook her head sadly as he left the house and headed for the Plaza, as though she wondered whatever possessed her son to behave in such weird ways.

Friday afternoons in the Plaza were busy. His rented car circled the block twice, then pulled into the parking lot across the street from the toy store. He wandered past shelves lined with tin soldiers and ready-to-assemble models of cars, planes, and boats.

"May I help you find something?" a young man asked politely.

Dan lifted his brows and mustered his courage. "I'm looking for the Barbie dolls," he murmured so softly the clerk had to ask him to repeat himself.

He melted with embarrassment when the clerk pointed to the area beyond the checkout counter and loudly announced, "Sir, the Barbie dolls are right over there." Probably no one cared, but he felt as though every eye in the place was focused on him, the weird man who was shopping for Barbie dolls. He slunk past the clerks busily ringing up sales and rounded the corner. Sure enough, there were the Barbies, dozens of them. No, *hundreds* of them, with cars, boats, beauty shops, grocery stores, RVs, clothes, purses, lunch boxes, and items too numerous for him to investigate. He scanned the shelves top to bottom, trying to decide what to buy for Becca.

"How about a Christmas Barbie for your daughter?" a nice lady wearing a name tag asked. "We just received a new shipment; every little girl wants those."

He started to explain that he didn't have a daughter, but

deciding it really was none of the woman's business, he just let her think what she wanted. Actually, he was enjoying this. He'd played parts before; why not that of a father? He cleared his throat casually. "A Christmas doll? I think my daughter would like that." Inside he was shaking as badly as if he were stealing the doll instead of merely faking a daddy disguise. This daddy stuff was harder than he'd expected.

He wanted to buy a Barbie for Carlee, too. But which one? It had to be special, very special. "And I'd like another doll, more special than the Christmas doll. A real fancy one adults would buy for themselves."

The clerk smiled and pointed to a circular, lighted case. "Any one of those dolls would do nicely," the smiling clerk said proudly. "Is your wife a collector?"

"Wife? No. . .er. . .yes, she is." He'd succeeded in his charade as a father; why not be a husband? "Yes, she has a rather extensive collection," he said with all the calmness he could gather, hoping his face didn't give away his deception.

"Oh, does she have the latest Bob Mackie?"

Dan rolled his eyes. "No, only Barbies. She doesn't collect male dolls."

"Sir," she said rather indignantly, "Bob Mackie designs gowns for the Bob Mackie designer line of Barbie dolls. They are very much in demand by the most discriminating buyers."

He lifted his chin and faked with authority, "I knew that. Just a little joke, you know."

With a bemused smile, she asked, "Then, sir, do you think your wife would like the *new* Bob Mackie Barbie doll? Or has she already added this exquisite doll to her collection?"

"I don't remember for sure," he said thoughtfully. "If I purchase it and she already has it, can she exchange it?"

The woman's mocking expression never changed. "Of course, sir. Just be sure to keep the receipt."

"Then I'll take both dolls. Gift-wrapped, please."

"Wouldn't you like to see the doll first, sir? Most of our customers want to see such an expensive doll before deciding to purchase it. We want you to be happy."

Expensive? How expensive could a little doll in a fancy dress be? "Yes, of course—I'd like to see it."

She carefully lifted an exquisitely dressed doll from the top shelf of the glass case and held it out for him to see. It was lovely. Even Dan could appreciate its beauty.

"This is one of Mr. Mackie's most unusual designs. And although it is the most expensive one yet, it's well worth the price of three hundred dollars. It's—"

Dan nearly strangled on her words. "Uh—did you say three hundred dollars?" He stared at the doll.

She reared back with a surprised look on her face. "Yes, I did. Surely you were aware of the cost of a Bob Mackie design since your wife is a collector!"

He faked a laugh. "I'm kidding again. Of course I'm aware of the price of a Bill Marker doll. I'll take it."

"Bob Mackie, sir. Bob Mackie."

Now his dander was up and with a stern face he answered, "I knew that. Bob Mackie. Isn't that what I said?"

"Whatever," the woman said flippantly. "If you'll follow me, we'll ring up your items and you may wait in one of those chairs over there while your purchases are being wrapped."

Dan registered a look of disgust. "I didn't say I was through."

She stopped in her tracks. "You want another doll?"

"No. A baseball. You do have baseballs, don't you?"

"Collector or to play with?" she asked coolly.

"Collector," he snapped.

"This way, sir."

Picking out the baseball wasn't nearly as hard as the Barbie dolls. He selected one with the name of a familiar player autographed on it. It was only thirty-five dollars and came in a hard plastic, see-through case—the perfect ball.

"I'll take it, and I'd like a second ball, a nice one that a boy can play with and not have to worry about losing it or getting it dirty."

When the clerk announced the total, Dan decided that being a husband and father could be a pretty expensive role.

"Thank you, sir. Your family is going to be very happy with the gifts you've purchased."

Dan smiled at the clerk, then exited the store with his selections tucked safely under an arm, his smile the width of his face. Shopping at the toy store had been an education, but he had to admit he'd loved every minute of it, especially the part he'd played as husband and father.

He saluted as he passed the huge stone teddy bear out front. "See you again someday, fella. If I ever have a wife and kids of my own, I'll keep your store in mind. Meantime, keep my secret, okay?"

He thought he saw the bear wink!

seven

The driver slowly pulled the rental car into the parking lot and dowsed its lights. The man behind the wheel stretched and checked his watch: five A.M. He twisted the dial until he found a country western station, leaned back against the headrest, closed his eyes, and began tapping his fingertips on the steering wheel to the beat of the music. A smile crossed his freshly shaven face as he thought of his shopping spree the day before, and he chuckled. What would Carlee think if she knew about his game of deception at the store? Dan Castleberry with a wife and kids? Now, *that* was a thought. He wondered if he'd really fooled the clerks. Probably. They didn't care who he was buying gifts for as long as his VISA card was good. When should he give them the presents? Maybe as a going-away gift. *His* going away.

Headlights passed quickly across his windshield as the minivan whipped into the lot and stopped next to his car. Carlee Bennett stepped out, her coat wrapped tightly about her to ward off the chill of the early morning winds. He wished she didn't have to work this early morning session, then realized she was there because of him. Otherwise, she'd be coming in an hour later.

She rapped on his window with her gloved hand. "Hey, in there! Trying to use up all your gas sitting in my lot?"

Quickly he flipped the key in the ignition and stepped out into the cold. "Naw, just waiting to see if you have any goodies for our coffee before I make up my mind to come in."

She grinned and held up a white plastic bag.

He wrapped his arm around her shoulder and fell in step as

they moved toward the door to escape the cold wind. While Dan carried the VCR into the ice arena to set it up for viewing, Carlee made coffee and retrieved his skates from her office. By now, their early morning routine was well established.

She loved having him there in the mornings. For four years, she had entered that blackened barn of a building by herself, and although she'd never told anyone, she'd been terrified. But thankfully, for the next few weeks she'd have Dan Castleberry waiting for her when she arrived.

"Five dollars for your thoughts."

Her daydream bubble burst at the sound of his voice.

"Did you say five dollars? I thought the price was a penny."

"Inflation."

"Corn-ee!" she shouted after him as he moved away.

Once seated in front of the VCR, she listened as his skates clicked across the ice in time to the music. And she watched to make sure his every move was in sync with the videotape.

At the end of the first routine, the skater showered her with the customary ice shavings, then hit the "Off" button on the tape player. He towered over her as she sat on the cold metal chair sipping her coffee. "Well, where is it?" he demanded playfully as he shaped his muscular body into the form of the Beast. "Give it to me—now!"

She pretended to be frightened as she lifted her arms to shield herself. "And what will you do if I don't?" she asked in a high-pitched voice.

His body hovered over her as he answered slowly in a low, mellow voice, "I will strangle all your Barbie dolls!"

"Oh, no," she said meekly in her normal voice. "I promised, didn't I?"

"Yep," he answered as he dropped into the chair beside her. "You promised, right in front of your children, that you'd show me your Barbie dolls after supper."

She pulled the bag from its hiding place under her chair.

"Could I buy a little redemption with a surprise cupcake?"

"Surprise cupcakes, eh?" he questioned as he thrust his hand into the bag. "What's the surprise part?" He twirled the little cake in his hand, pulled the paper off and took a teensy bite. "Good, but no surprise."

A crooked smile graced her lips.

He took another bite, bigger this time. "Hmm, marshmallow."

She loved these morning snack times. The two had so much fun. And no matter what she served him, he loved it.

"More," he commanded once again in his Beast voice and stance after he'd devoured the first cake. "Me want more!"

She rolled her eyes and handed him the entire bag.

He flashed those dimples and plowed into a second cake. She loved his sense of humor, his easygoing manner.

"If you don't ease up on those cupcakes, you won't be able to skate," she warned as he popped a third one into his mouth and followed it with a swish of coffee.

"Okay, okay. I get the message. Back to work, right?"

"Right!"

At 6:15, the patchers and their mothers arrived, right on time. Dan hung around and helped Carlee sweep and clean the snack bar and get it ready for the day. Mrs. Sweeney, who operated the snack bar, was visiting her daughter. Her sister was coming in to replace her but couldn't make it until 9:30. Carlee had told her not to worry—she'd make sure the snack bar was ready for the day.

"You're pretty adept at sweeping," she commented, remembering the sweeping job he'd accepted on her front porch.

"Learned it in the Navy, swabbing decks."

She stopped her work. "You were in the Navy?"

"Not exactly," he quipped with that ornery grin that brought out his dimples. "Skated the part of a sailor in a show."

She tossed a damp sponge toward him and he caught it in

midair. "Then swab, swabbie," she commanded.

It was amazing how much faster the work went when the load was shared. In no time the snack bar was shipshape. The "sailor" had done a good job.

Carlee poured two fresh cupfuls of steaming coffee and carried them to one of the round tables that circled the snack bar. "Dan, I don't get it. Here you are the lead skater in one of the best-known ice shows in the country, maybe the world, yet you come into my home and eat hot dogs. You play with my children. Now you clean our snack bar. Why?"

Dan smoothed his paper napkin and placed his cup squarely in the center, then raised his eyes to meet hers. "Carlee, to be real honest, I don't know why. I only know that I've enjoyed myself this week, and being here in Kansas City, more than I'd ever dreamed possible."

"You mean because of your folks? And the practicing?"

He leaned back in the chair and balanced it precariously on its hind legs. "No, I've hardly seen my folks. Their lives are much too busy to include me. And the practicing? I could have done that in Florida, like the rest of the cast."

Dan reached across the table and cradled both her hands in his. "It's you, Carlee. It's your family. It's this place. It's magical. I can't explain it to you. I only know that this has been one of the happiest weeks of my life, yet I haven't done a thing that's outstanding. Maybe you can explain it to me." He squeezed her hand appreciatively.

She pulled back, unsure how to interpret what he'd said.

Two patchers sidled up to the counter and tapped the little brass bell for service. Carlee left Dan sitting alone and went to wait on the girls. When she turned, he was gone.

It was pleasant to see the sun shining brightly as she locked the door behind her at the end of the morning session and strolled briskly to her minivan. A flutter on her windshield caught her attention; a note was anchored beneath the wipers. She flipped the blade aside and read:

I'd like to take you and the kids to dinner and a movie
tonight. See you at 5:00. Call me if you can't make it.
Dan

Of course she could make it! She folded the note and
slipped it into her pocket. And she knew the children would
be thrilled when she told them about Dan's invitation.

❧

Dan Castleberry found a note, too, from his mother. It was
taped to his bedroom door when he arrived home. He was to
call Brad in Florida, as soon as possible.

Brad, his closest friend, was also a featured skater in the
show. Dan phoned immediately. Brad and his fiancée had
decided to get married the next Tuesday, in Florida, and he
wanted Dan to be his best man. Dan assured him he'd be
there. He'd never let his old friend down.

He phoned the airline and made his reservation.

❧

The house was quiet when Carlee stepped into her kitchen at
noon. Bobby tiptoed in to meet her. "Mama, Becca doesn't
feel good. Grandma said she's gotta fever. She's hot!"

Carlee rushed into the family room and found her daughter
nestled in Mother Bennett's arms in the rocking chair. She
took the flushed child from Ethel and held her close. "Baby,
baby. What's the matter with Mama's baby?"

Their grandmother stood by silently as her daughter-in-law
cradled the child and strode about the room, planting kisses
on the four-year-old's hot little cheeks. "I took her temperature; it was not quite a hundred. Do you think she's cutting
more teeth?" Ethel asked gently.

Carlee smiled and nodded her head as she lowered herself
into the softly padded chair and began to rock; it was the

same chair her beloved Robert had been rocked in when he was a child.

Ethel backed away quietly with a slight wave. "Call me if you need anything. I'm going home to fix lunch for Jim."

The young mother rocked her daughter for the next few hours as Bobby exchanged cool, damp washcloths to cool Becca's brow. He was such a helper, wringing out the cloths with his strong little hands, then placing them on his sister's petite forehead. Carlee wanted to hug her son, too, but he was too busy being her little man.

At four o'clock, Becca's fever broke and her tiny body cooled off. Her eyes were still droopy, but Carlee knew the worst was over. More than likely, it had been the teeth.

"Now can we go to McDonald's for supper?" Bobby asked as he gathered up the wet clothes. "Becca's feeling better."

"Supper!" his mother shouted as she put her hand to her forehead. "Oh, no! I completely forgot—Dan wanted to take us out for supper and a movie."

"Yeah! Let's go!" Bobby cheered joyfully.

Carlee clamped her hand over her son's wrist. "Sorry, Bobby, we can't go; it's too soon for Becca."

Bobby's laugh turned to a frown. "Oh, Mama. Please?"

"We can't go, honey. Maybe Dan'll take us another time. Be a good boy and bring Mama the phone."

When Dan answered on the second ring, she explained about Becca's fever and asked for a rain check.

"No rain check!" he declared firmly. "But let me bring supper and a movie to you and the kids. Okay?"

"Really, Dan? You don't have to do this, you know." She should have known he would respond in such a thoughtful way; it was so like the man she'd come to know and care for.

"Do the kids like the Colonel's chicken?"

"It's one of their favorites."

"Then, chicken it is. I'll be there around five. Can I pick

up a prescription or anything?"

Carlee smiled. "No. Just the chicken. Thanks anyway."

Bobby leaped through the house, swinging his arms wildly. "Dan's coming, Becca! Dan's coming!"

Becca raised her flushed face from her mother's shoulder with interest. "Is he, Mama? Will Dan hold me?"

Carlee lifted the damp little ringlets that encircled Becca's pink face and pushed them from her forehead. "Yes, baby. I'm sure Dan will hold you. Just get well, okay?"

The baby lowered her head onto her mother's breast.

When the doorbell chimed, Bobby ran to open the door. There stood Dan with a winsome smile on his face. He held two large sacks with colorful caricatures of the Colonel on their sides. Becca lifted her head when Dan came into the room and gave him a weak little wave and whispered, "Hi, Dan."

"How's my girl?" he asked as he placed his big hand on her clammy forehead. "Dan doesn't like Becca to be sick."

"Fine," came a tiny voice. She looked up and blinked slowly. "Hold me, Dan."

"Sure, honey. Dan'll hold you." He bent and kissed a rosy little cheek. "But don't you think we should eat first? Dan brought you some nice fried chicken. Your big brother is going to help me put the food on the coffee table—if it's okay with your mom." He shot a questioning glance at Carlee, who nodded her permission. "Then as soon as supper is over, Dan'll hold you for as long as you want." He stroked the little girl's hair lovingly.

"Yeah," Bobby agreed as he began taking the boxes and plastic utensils out of the bags and placing them on the table. "Dan and me are gonna fix supper for you girls."

The two *men* put cartons of coleslaw, baked beans, and mashed potatoes on the table next to the boxes of chicken, along with paper plates, napkins, and the utensils.

"Dan! You bought so much!" Carlee exclaimed when she saw the feast placed before them. "There's no way the four of us can eat all of this! You'll have to come back and help us eat the leftovers."

He smiled shyly. "I thought you'd never ask!"

The four enjoyed the impromptu fried chicken dinner. Even Becca nibbled on a chicken leg, but it was the mashed potatoes she enjoyed most. They barely made a dent in all the food. Dan suggested they make up a box for Bobby to take over to the Bennetts; the remainder was stuffed into the refrigerator for another day.

"That was thoughtful of you, Dan, sending that box over to my in-laws. Thank you for thinking of it."

"No problem. Just making brownie points."

Before she could question his comment, he changed the subject. "I thought about getting a videotape of *Robin Hood* for Bobby, but I knew Becca wouldn't like that. Then I thought about getting a tape of *The Little Mermaid* for Becca, but I knew Bobby wouldn't like that. So. . ." Dan moved to the coat closet, reached into his overcoat, and pulled a videotape from each pocket. "I got 'em both!"

Bobby cheered loudly. Little Becca's eyes brightened. Dan handed the videotapes to Bobby, then lifted Becca carefully from her mother's arms and carried her to the comfy old sofa, gently lowering himself into its corner.

Bobby loaded Becca's tape first and the four of them watched *The Little Mermaid* while the little girl lay motionless in Dan's lap. Occasionally, she'd lift her face toward his and slip a warm little hand around his neck. He'd kiss one baby cheek and then the other, then each eyelid. She'd smile and go back to watching her video. By the end of the movie, she was sound asleep and her temperature was normal.

"Let me put her to bed," Carlee offered as she moved to take her baby from Dan's strong arms.

He shook his head. "No, let me do it." He carried Becca to her room and placed her carefully between the Barbie sheets, then tucked the pink comforter up under her chin before leaning to kiss her face.

"You should have a family of your own, Dan. You're great with kids."

"Just *your* kids," he said wistfully as he slipped an arm around her waist and walked her into the family room where Bobby was watching *Robin Hood*. They sat on the sofa, side by side, until the tape ended. Dan tucked Bobby into bed for the night and knelt on one knee beside the boy while the child prayed. When he came back into the family room, he walked directly to Carlee, took her by the hand, lifted her to her feet, and ordered, "Now, show me your Barbie dolls!"

She tilted her head to one side in question. "You're sure you want to see them? They're not exactly a guy thing."

"Positive. Lead on," he told her with a mocking grin.

She led him through her bedroom to a large walk-in closet and switched on the light. He thought he was back at the toy store! Shelves lined the walls along one side, and on them were more than a hundred Barbie dolls, all in unopened boxes. He quickly scanned the shelves looking for the Bob Mackie doll and was relieved when he didn't find it there.

"They're not opened?" he questioned with surprise.

She winced. "Bite your tongue! Of course not! It depreciates their value if they're opened. I only purchase dolls in perfect boxes. You know, mint condition."

He let out a long, low whistle as he moved along the shelves. "Where did you get all these?"

"Some I get when I travel, which isn't often. Most of them Father Bennett has brought home to me when he's attended skating championships. Others have been birthday and Christmas presents. They're all special to me." She lovingly brushed her fingertips across the top of the box with an oval front that rested at the end of the top row, and pulled it from the shelf. "She's the one who started it all—the 1988 Holiday Barbie. Robert bought it for me for Christmas that year as a joke, but I loved it. The next year I bought the 1989 Holiday Barbie as soon as it was released, and I've been collecting Barbies ever since. See? All my Holidays are lined up together on the top shelf. When Christmas comes, I'll display them in the family room, right along with the other decorations. Don't you dare laugh, Dan Castleberry!"

Dan symbolically crossed his heart with the index finger of his right hand. "I won't; I promise! Are the Christmas dolls the fanciest ones they make?" he asked, hiding his new-found education on collector Barbie dolls.

"Oh, my, no!" Carlee pulled a lovely bride doll from a lower shelf. "See this one? It's a bride doll and its dress is by a designer named Bob Mackie. His are some of the most expensive dolls in the Barbie line. I have only this one, but there are a number of others by now. I had to have at least one Bob Mackie, and I won't even begin to tell you how much I paid for her. You'd never believe it!"

"Wow," he uttered as he looked at the beautiful doll clad in white, feeling a bit smug about his recent doll purchases. Soon, the newest Bob Mackie would be joining the beautiful bride doll. He could hardly wait to see Carlee's face when he gave it to her, confident he'd made the right selection. Somehow, the cost had become instantly insignificant.

Carlee pulled several other dolls from the shelves and explained about them to Dan. He listened intently as they moved from doll to doll. He loved the excitement in Carlee's voice as she talked about her collection.

She shoved the last doll back onto the shelf and grabbed both his hands in hers. "Don't say I didn't keep my promise. And, yes! I do have more Barbies than Becca. Satisfied?"

Dan gave her hands a quick squeeze. "Satisfied! I guess

it's time I let you get to bed. You've had a long, hard day. Tell you what; I'm going to skip my practice session tomorrow morning. It's Sunday and you deserve a break. That way, you won't have to leave Becca."

She tucked her hand into Dan's and walked him to the door. "Thanks, Dan; you're a good friend. It meant a lot to the children to have you come over tonight. They would have loved to see you—with or without supper." She tightened her grip on his arm before opening the front door. "Good night. See you at Mother and Father Bennett's for lunch."

He stood in the doorway and looked into her round blue eyes. "You're quite a lady, Carlee Bennett." He bent and kissed her on the top of her head and lightly nuzzled her hair with his chin; it smelled like gardenias. He had an overwhelming urge to kiss her. She was so close; it would be so easy to take her into his arms. His lips nuzzled her hair again as she stood motionless; he was sure he could hear her heart beating. With one finger beneath her chin, he lifted her face to his and gazed into those beautiful clear-blue eyes. Why didn't she say something? Anything? Slowly, he lowered his lips to her forehead, as gently as if he were kissing Becca's warm cheeks.

She just stood there.

He wrapped his arms about her and drew her to him. He half expected her to push him away, slap him, maybe tell him to leave. But, instead, she seemed to melt into his arms and welcome his embrace.

"Dan. . ."

He touched a finger to her lips. "Shh. Don't say it."

She leaned into his strong chest. Her arms lifted to encircle his neck as they stood there looking into one another's eyes.

"I need a drink of water," little Becca called out in her loud baby voice as she stood in the doorway in her jammies, the unclothed doll in her hand.

Carlee pushed away from Dan with a look of embarrassment. "Sorry. Becca needs me."

Dan smiled. "So do I, Carlee."

With Becca's untimely entrance, he'd forgotten to tell Carlee about Brad's wedding.

eight

Dan woke at 6:00. Besides having trouble getting Carlee off his mind, he was worried about Becca. The little girl had looked so pale when he'd carried her to bed last night. He wanted to call to see how she was feeling, but it was too early. He hoped the children all felt fine and Carlee was sleeping in a little later than usual.

It was seven A.M. in Florida where his friend lived, so he decided to call him instead. A sleepy voice answered. Dan tried to explain who was calling, and that he had made reservations to fly into Florida on Monday and would be there in plenty of time for the wedding on Tuesday, but he wondered if the message ever soaked into his friend's sleepy brain.

After fixing himself a cup of instant coffee, he wandered through the living and dining rooms of his parents' house and closely examined the abstract paintings that graced the walls. Each had been purchased as an investment, yet his parents hated them. Their only merit was the signature in the corner that provided their monetary value. Suddenly he hated them, too.

The ugly collection of abstract paintings cried out, *Look at me. I'm valuable! I'm expensive!* But Carlee's collection of dolls said, *Come share Carlee's love for me. Let me take you into fantasyland. I'm here for you to enjoy, to hold, and to appreciate.* At any price they were worth the cost. He chuckled to himself and said aloud, "Even the three-hundred-dollar one with the Bill Markham design!" How he wished his mother would enter Carlee's closet and become like a child again, learning anew how to enjoy the simple things of life.

He waited till 9:00, then dialed Carlee's number. "Bobby, how's Becca?" he asked with sincere concern.

"She's fine. Mama's dressing her for Sunday school."

Dan felt a surge of relief. "Can I speak to your mother, please?" He heard a clunk as Bobby placed the phone on the table and went in search of his mother.

"Good morning, Dan. Would you believe Becca is feeling like her old self and chattering a mile a minute this morning?"

"Well, I won't keep you—don't want to make you late for Sunday school. I just wanted to know how Becca is; I was worried about her. See you at two at the Bennetts'."

As if on impulse she asked, "Come with us, Dan! To church, I mean. It doesn't start till 10:45. You have plenty of time!"

He hesitated, then reluctantly answered, "Naw. I haven't been to church since I was a teenager. I don't know the routine; I might embarrass you."

She laughed. "Haven't I been coaching your skating? I can coach you through the church service so you don't make any mistakes. Please. The children would be thrilled if I could tell them you'll be there." She paused. "I'd like it, too."

He teetered on the brink of saying yes.

"I'll send the kids on to Sunday school with their grandparents and wait for you here so we can go together."

He was convinced. "Okay, pick you up at 10:20. But don't expect me to make a habit of this."

⁂

Dan Castleberry adjusted the rearview mirror. He was slightly nervous at the thought of attending church but looking forward to spending more time with the Bennett family. In the car's trunk, he'd placed the three gift-wrapped packages.

Carlee waved through the picture window when he drove into her driveway, then rushed to the door to meet him.

He took her hands in his and stood back and admired her

from head to toe. "Wow, do you look terrific! You don't look like the mother of two feisty kids!"

Her cheeks flushed. She seemed to blush quite often since she'd met Dan Castleberry. "And, what's a mother of two supposed to look like?"

"Not like you! You look—like a model."

"Dan," she asked coyly with a wink, "didn't your mother tell you your nose would grow each time you told a lie?"

"Been there. Done that," he retorted with a smirk.

"What's that supposed to mean? I don't get it."

Hands on his hips, he grinned that crooked little smile of his. "I skated as Pinocchio. My nose did grow—with a little help from the makeup department."

"You're incorrigible," she chastised. "And, we'd better get going; the kids are probably driving Ethel crazy."

&

Two eager children stood in the church's vestibule, watching for Dan and their mother. When the couple stepped into the church, Becca burst from her grandfather's hold, leaped into Dan's arms, and hugged him tightly. "I love you, Dan," she said as she snuggled her face into his neck.

Bobby took Dan's free hand and dragged him over to meet his grandmother.

"You've made quite an impression on my grandchildren and husband, Mr. Castleberry. I've heard nice things about you."

Now it was his turn to blush. "And you, Mrs. Bennett. Carlee has told me how unselfish you are, what a friend you've been to her, and what a wonderful grandmother you are to the children. But please—call me Dan. The kids do."

"Then, Dan it is! We'll expect you at our house around two o'clock." She patted his shoulder, then disappeared.

Jim Bennett extended his right hand as he leaned toward Dan. "She has a great dinner cooking. Come hungry!"

Carlee led Dan and the children into a back pew. It was

obvious she was trying to make his church experience as comfortable as possible. People all around leaned close to say hello and to welcome him to their church. He was surprised at how comfortable he felt with these strangers. And he was proud to be accompanied by such a beautiful young woman and her very special children.

Becca refused to get off Dan's lap when Carlee tried to take her from him, and he was no help; he hugged the little girl even tighter. When they stood to sing the first hymn, Bobby moved past his mother to Dan's other side and snuggled in close to the big man when they sat down. The beautiful sanctuary, the stained-glass windows, the cushioned pews, the thickly carpeted floors—all seemed to say "welcome" with their beauty and warmth.

When the service was over, they moved out into the lobby with the other churchgoers, who smiled at them with friendly faces and extended hands of welcome. The pastor told them how glad he was that they were there and complimented Carlee on the regular attendance of her family as he shook Dan's hand warmly.

"Now, was that so bad?" Carlee asked when they climbed into Dan's car and headed for home.

"It was okay, I guess," Dan answered without enthusiasm.

Bobby looked crushed. "You didn't like it?"

Dan reached over the back of the seat and poked the boy in the arm. "Just kidding. Of course I liked it. But I'm not sure I could take a steady diet of it, like you and your mom."

Bobby slipped two skinny arms around Dan's neck. "Well, I liked having you there with us."

Dan patted the eight-year-old's hands. "I liked being there with you too. I like being with your family anywhere."

Becca look slighted, like she wanted Dan's attention too. "I love you, Dan," she called out in her loud voice from her place in the backseat.

Dan felt a lump rise in his throat. Not even his parents said those words to him. In fact, other than Bobby and Becca, he couldn't remember anyone saying they loved him since his grandmother died. It touched him deeply, but he attempted to conceal that fact; such tender emotions were so foreign to him.

When they reached Carlee's home, Dan helped his passengers to the door then excused himself, explaining he needed to get something from the car. When he returned, he was carrying the three gift-wrapped packages. The children danced happily around him. "Are they for us?"

Carlee looked embarrassed. Dan only laughed and enjoyed their childish enthusiasm.

He ordered the group to be seated on the sofa in the family room, then placed a bright yellow package with a green polka-dotted ribbon in Becca's lap. "Open it, honey," he told the smiling child as he knelt before her.

"Dan!" Carlee acknowledged with a frown. "None of us has a birthday. Why did you do this?"

He looked at the happy faces of the children and answered, "Because I wanted to. That's why! Now, Mama, be quiet and let me have some fun."

Becca pulled the paper with one big jerk and squealed when she caught sight of the beautiful Christmas Holiday Barbie. She ripped the doll from the box and hugged it to her and ran into Dan's waiting arms. "Thank you, Dan." She squeezed his neck and kissed his cheek.

"You're welcome, Becca." His heart was nearly bursting with joy at seeing Becca's cute little face express so much happiness.

Carlee's eyes took on a misty look. "Oh, Dan. The Holiday doll."

He placed the package with the cowboys on blue wrapping paper in Bobby's lap. "This is for you, Bobby."

The boy was a little more patient than his sister; he carefully pulled the ribbon and tape from the package before opening the box. He stared at the two balls, then at Dan.

"One for keeping, one for playing," Dan answered without being asked as he watched the boy's reaction to his gift.

Bobby picked up the see-through box and read the autograph. "Thank you, Dan. This is the best ball I've ever seen. Boy, wait'll my coach sees this." He held the box as if it would break and uttered "Wow" over and over.

"The other one is for playing catch. Maybe you and I can do that sometime before I leave. Would you like that?"

The boy ran to Dan and hugged him around the waist. "Yes, I'd like it. Playing catch with you would be the best present ever. Thank you, Dan."

Dan placed the package wrapped in pink foil with a pink bow in the young mother's lap. "Mama, this is for you. Open it."

She lifted weepy eyes to his. "I can't, Dan. You've done so much for me—*us*—already."

He touched her cheek. "Carlee, would you refuse my gift? When I went to all the trouble of selecting it just for you?"

"But. . .Dan. . ."

"Carlee, please open it."

She appeared to be reluctant as she untied the bow and removed the wrapping paper. He was glad they'd put the doll's original box into a plain white one before wrapping it; it prolonged the fun of watching her open the package. As she lifted the lid, she burst into tears at the sight of the beautiful doll. "Oh, Dan! A Bob Mackie!"

"Yep, the new one. Have you seen it?" he asked with pride.

She held the doll at arm's length. "No—oh, it's so beautiful!" She lowered it and put it back into the box.

"What are you doing, Carlee? Don't you like it?" Dan

grabbed her hands to stop her as she shoved it away.

"I can't accept a gift like this, Dan. I know this doll was very expensive."

Dan lifted the doll's box and placed it back in her lap. "Carlee, I bought it for you; I want you to have it. I could've bought a cheaper doll, but I wanted you to have this one. This doll is yours and I won't take no for an answer."

The young woman sniffled and rubbed at her eyes with her sleeves. "But, Dan—"

"No buts, Carlee!" he said in a soft but firm voice as he pulled a fresh hankie from his pocket and handed it to her. "And if you want to take her out of her box, I won't tell a soul!"

She laughed through her tears, then blew her nose on the hankie. "Oh, Dan. Didn't I do a good job educating you? Little girls open their doll boxes! Big girls don't!"

He seated himself beside her on the sofa. "You did an excellent job educating me; you just did it too late. I'd already bought these dolls before you showed me your collection. I was sure relieved to learn neither you nor Becca had the new Christmas doll and that you had no plans of buying the new Bill Maxwell doll."

Carlee giggled through eyes that sparkled with tears. "Bob Mackie, Dan! Bob Mackie!" She kissed him quickly on the cheek. "Thank you, Dan. I love her! I'll keep her forever!"

Little Becca yanked at his sleeve. "Can you help me, Dan? I can't get Barbie's shoes off the cardboard."

He gave Carlee's hand a squeeze, then dropped on his knees before the little girl and began to work on the plastic ties holding the doll's shoes fast. When he'd finished that project, he pulled the certificate of authenticity from the autographed ball's box and read it to Bobby, who listened with rapt attention.

Carlee watched him intently. He was an attractive man in

his muted brown tweed sport coat. Dan was a sharp dresser. He was used to gracious living. Everything about him reflected the affluent lifestyle with which he'd grown up. Yet here he sat in her home, playing with her children. And, best of all, he had attended church with them.

He smoothed his hair where tiny fingers had tangled it. "What are you thinking? You look miles away from us."

"You. The kids. Thinking how lucky we are to have a friend like you." She patted him on the knee and rose to her feet. "It's nearly two; they'll be looking for us."

The four made their way, hand in hand, across the lawn that joined the two Bennett houses. Father Bennett greeted them at the door. "Welcome! Welcome!" he said as he encouraged Dan to remove his jacket and make himself at home.

Carlee excused herself, and she and Becca hurried into the kitchen to help Ethel with the last-minute preparations.

"Look, Grandpa," Bobby said proudly as he followed his grandfather and Dan into the den. He produced the baseball from the little backpack that he wore everywhere he went. It contained all the things he loved most—a broken pocket watch, a picture of his father, a handheld video game. "Dan gave it to me. It's not even my birthday."

Jim took the clear plastic box from the boy's hand and examined it closely. "Well, I'd say this is some present. Dan must like you a lot to give you something this nice!" He nodded knowingly toward Dan. "And expensive!" When Jim finished reading, he slipped the paper and ball into its box and handed it to Bobby, who rushed off to show his grandmother.

Jim locked his hands behind his head and leaned back in the chair. "That was mighty nice of you, Dan. Meant a lot to Bobby to have you give him a present like that—for no reason at all." The older man closed his eyes and breathed a sigh. "What that boy needs is a father."

Dan nodded at his new friend's words. "Does Carlee ever

date?" he blurted out. "I mean, does she have a boyfriend?"

Jim's eyes widened, and he looked long and hard at Dan before answering. "No, she doesn't date or have a boyfriend, although we've done everything we can to encourage her. She needs a life of her own; she's a beautiful young woman." He added with a smile, "In case you hadn't noticed. But, she isn't interested in men. Says there isn't a man alive who would love her and the children the way Robert did. She may be right. They were the perfect couple."

Dan flinched. "I'd think men would be beating a path to her door."

Jim rubbed his chin. "They have been. She isn't interested. Her standards are high, and the guy'd have to be pretty special to live up to them. It's a heavy burden to raise two children alone. We try to help as much as we can, but she's an independent little gal."

"I've noticed that," Dan interjected. "She's quite a woman. Never met another one like her."

"Lucky the man that catches her, Dan. She'll make someone a wonderful wife. That girl is as special as they come." He stopped speaking when Carlee entered the room.

"Mom Bennett sent me to fetch you two hungry men; everything is on the table. The kids are already seated."

They followed obediently as the delicious smells from the dining room beckoned. Dan pulled the chair out for Carlee. Jim tried to lift Becca, to put her in her booster seat as he'd done hundreds of times, but she pulled away from him. "I want Dan to help me, Grandpa!"

Dan rushed around the table and lifted the smiling baby into the seat, then pushed her chair close to the table. Becca grinned and blinked her long lashes in his direction.

Bobby gave Dan a toothy grin as the boy slipped his hand into his new friend's hand. Carlee smiled and leaned forward as her hand slid into Dan's other hand, and the family circle was complete as Jim bowed his head and began to pray.

"Lord, we thank You for providing this food for us and for Ethel who prepared it. We thank You for Dan, Carlee, Bobby, and Becca being with us at our table to share in Your bounty. We ask Your continued blessing in the name of Your Son. And we praise You."

Collectively, they all said, "Amen."

As a family, they laughed, joked, and enjoyed Ethel's wonderful meal. Dan stole a glance around the table at the happy faces. He couldn't remember the last time he'd had a home-cooked meal like this. Never at his parents' house. The cook had prepared the meals when he was a child, and now their meals were all eaten out in a fine restaurant or at the country club. This was, without a doubt, the best meal he'd ever tasted, and he told his hostess so.

"I'm glad you enjoy my cooking," Ethel said bashfully, embarrassed by his lavish praise.

"He likes Mama's hot dogs, too," little Becca announced proudly as she licked the butter from her second roll.

Her grandmother placed her hand on the tiny girl's shoulder with pride. "Your mother is a wonderful cook, Becca. She knows how to prepare far more than hot dogs."

Carlee threw her head back with a laugh and winked at her mother-in-law. "I must be a good cook; I learned everything I know from you—and you're terrific!"

With that, Jim stood up with his hands extended in the air. "Enough of this mutual admiration society. I suggest we wait on our dessert until later." Then, pointing to Dan and Bobby, he added, "We menfolk will build a nice fire in the fireplace while the ladies do up the kitchen. That okay with everyone?"

They agreed unanimously and headed for their designated jobs, full and happy.

🍃

When the women joined them in the family room twenty

minutes later, they found Jim asleep in one recliner and Dan, with Bobby in his lap in the other, reading the Sunday sports section. The rest of the newspaper lay scattered on the floor at their feet. A tear forced its way down Carlee's cheek. How much her children had missed, having been robbed of their father's presence in their lives.

&

Late in the afternoon, the foursome walked back across the lawn. Carlee put Becca down for a much-needed nap, while Dan popped the Odyssey tape into the VCR for Bobby.

There he was, waiting for her on the sofa, when she came back into the room with two cups of freshly made coffee.

"You're spoiling me, you know." He took the cup and motioned for her to sit beside him.

"Enjoy it while you can," she said with a balmy smile. "You have only two more weeks—the first one is gone!"

"Not quite two weeks," he corrected dismally.

She frowned. "What do you mean?"

He told her all about his friend Brad and the wedding.

Her frown turned to a look of sadness. "When will you be back?"

"Don't know. I haven't made return reservations yet."

Disappointment crossed her face. "Oh," she said softly.

Dan didn't know what to say; he hadn't expected a negative reaction. He'd thought she would be glad to get a little extra sleep the few mornings he'd be gone.

"Thursday's Thanksgiving. The children and I were hoping you'd spend the day with us. You know, a turkey and all the fixings. I was going to cook for you." She lowered her gaze to the floor, apparently wishing she hadn't mentioned her plans.

He took her hand in his and pressed it gently. "You don't have to do that for me. Won't Ethel and Jim be expecting you and the children for Thanksgiving?"

She drew back slightly. "No, they're going to St. Louis to be with Ethel's sister and her husband."

"If I'd known. . ."

She gnawed at her lower lip. "It's okay. Really."

Dan lifted her chin with one finger and looked into her sapphire-blue eyes. "What if I come back Wednesday?"

That sparkle he loved so much returned to her face. "I wouldn't want you to change your plans for us."

"What do you mean 'for us'? I'd rather be here with the three of you for Thanksgiving than anyplace I can think of." He bent and playfully kissed her on the forehead. "Honest."

"Your parents are welcome to come with you."

Dan threw his head back with a robust laugh. "And miss the holiday buffet? To be with their only son? Surely you jest!" Their attitudes and lack of interest hurt him more than he cared to admit, even to himself.

"Dan, really. Do what works best for you. The children and I are used to being alone. We'll survive." If she were trying to mask her disappointment, she was doing a very poor job of it. It showed on her face.

"I *will* be back on Wednesday, and I'm honored to accept your invitation for Thanksgiving dinner." He stepped back dramatically and added, "If you promise you won't burn the turkey."

Carlee grabbed two pillows from the sofa and pelted him. He tried to duck, but she'd taken him by complete surprise. He quickly encircled her waist with his strong arms and held her tight. He could kiss her again so easily—she was so close, so desirable. Her lovely face was so near. . . .

Bobby looked up from his place on the floor, frowned, and said in a loud, authoritative voice, "No roughhousing in the family room!"

nine

One suitcase and one garment bag rested on the backseat of Dan Castleberry's rented car as he absentmindedly made his way toward the Ice Palace. He knew he was early, but he hadn't slept well. Was it the excitement of going back to be with his friends and the other cast members? Perhaps it was his leaving Carlee? A frown dug into his forehead. Maybe it was the three huge helpings of mashed potatoes and gravy or the four monstrous slices of roast beef. Or the two pieces of lemon meringue pie. He'd certainly eaten his share of Ethel's cooking, and then some.

So Brad was getting married. Maybe Brad was ready for it, but Dan wondered how a marriage could survive all the traveling. And the temptations. Brad skated pair numbers with many beautiful women. And his wife would continue to skate with the men in the cast. Dan wasn't sure he'd want *his* wife skating in skimpy costumes with any of those guys. He knew them too well—knew how they talked about women.

His *wife?* A smile came to his lips. He'd be an old man by the time he married, at the rate he was going. *If* he ever married. He was surprised to find Carlee's empty minivan already parked when he turned into the lot. He'd barely turned off the headlights when the rink's door flew open and she came running out, screaming and shaking uncontrollably, terror etched on her face. She flew into his arms and clung tightly, her speech erratic and garbled.

"There's a man in there! I–I saw him!" she screamed breathlessly.

Dan shoved her into the car and pulled the cellular phone

80

from the glove compartment. He dialed 911 and quickly gave them the details. "Did you recognize him? Is he still in there?"

Carlee held tightly onto his arm as she shook her head. "No! I never saw him before! He just stood there and looked at me when I turned on the lights! I ran!" Her voice trembled with fear and her face was deathly pale.

"You stay here. I'm going inside," he commanded as he broke her grasp and shoved her into his car.

She grabbed at his jacket. "No, Dan! Don't! Wait for the police!"

He pressed the lock button, slammed the door, and ordered, "Stay in the car and don't open the doors for anyone!" He moved quickly to the trunk and removed a flashlight and jack handle and headed for the rink as Carlee watched, her face a mask of fear.

The overhead lights were still glowing when he entered the big building, but no one was in sight. He knew that if Carlee said she saw someone, someone was there. Where could he be? Was he watching from some hidden area?

Maintaining a cool head, Dan headed for the office, where the previous day's receipts were kept until they could be counted and banked. The man might be anywhere in the building, he realized, but the office would be the most likely place for him to go if money were his goal.

The lights were off in the office, but the door was ajar. Dan knew Carlee always kept it locked. Silently he slipped his hand inside the door and switched on the lights. No one was in sight, but the lock for the heavy steel cabinet where she kept the cash box had been pried off. Dan lifted the jack handle over his head and moved as stealthily as a cat on the prowl to the closet where he had stored his skates. If someone were still in the office, the closet was the only place large enough for a man to conceal himself.

What should he do? If he waited for the police to check out the closet and the guy wasn't in there, he'd be wasting precious time and the guy might get away. Or worse, he might see Carlee waiting in the car and go after her. No, he couldn't take a chance on that; he had no choice but to check out that closet. He crept toward the door, his heart pounding. With one hand on the knob and the other gripping the jack handle, he yanked open the door and found a scared, skinny young man crouched on the floor, the cash box tucked securely under his arm.

Dan raised the jack handle over his head with both hands and fire in his eyes. "One move and I'll split your head open with this thing! If you think I'm kidding, try me. I'm aching for a reason to let you have it!" He was serious and he meant business. He knew if the kid were armed, he might go for his gun and he'd have to hit him. And he wondered, could he actually split another person's head open? If he had to? He hoped the police would arrive and he wouldn't have to find out. But, as the vision of Carlee running and screaming into his arms flashed through his mind, he knew if he had to, he could. He'd do anything to protect her. If the guy made one move, just one, he'd use the iron.

The wail of approaching sirens could be heard, and within seconds, two police cars wheeled into the parking lot and screeched to a halt. Three officers jumped out, pulled their guns from their holsters, and moved cautiously toward the open door. The fourth officer ran to Dan's car to question the frightened Carlee. Dan heard them enter and called out in a loud voice as he hovered over the man, "We're in here. In the office. It's okay; I've got him!"

When the officers entered the room, they found Dan, still poised with the jack handle over his head, ready to strike the man on the floor of the closet if provoked.

"Good work, young man," one of the officers told Dan

after they'd cuffed the perpetrator.

"But pretty stupid!" another officer added with a frown. "You could've been hurt, maybe even shot, coming in here like that. That guy might have been armed."

The first officer came to Dan's defense. "Hey, go easy on him. If this guy'd frightened my wife like that, I'd have gone after him too. So would you and you know it!"

Dan smiled nervously, his adrenaline pumping furiously. *Wife? No, sir. Not me!* he thought.

❧

Carlee waited nervously in the car. *What was going on in there?* She gasped with relief as she spotted the man, his hands on top of his head, being led from the building by the three officers, followed closely by Dan, who was unharmed. She ran to him and wrapped her arms about his neck.

"You should be proud of your husband," the officer said. "He had the guy cornered; all we had to do was cuff him. Sure great to see a man lay his life on the line to protect his wife like that—even though he should've waited for us."

She tried to explain that Dan was only a friend, but they were too busy shoving the burglar into the police car to hear her.

After they'd gone, Dan grinned and pulled her into his arms and held her still-shaking body. "Let them think what they will—I don't care. I'm just glad you're safe." Then, with a wink of his eye, he added, "Remember when I said if you were a good girl Santa might bring you a Barbie? Well, this Santa has decided what you really need is a German shepherd!"

Once they were in the rink with the door bolted, Carlee phoned Jim Bennett to let him know what had happened. "Dan saved my life, Father Bennett! No telling what that man might have done if Dan hadn't been there when I came running out of the building. I was sure the thief was right behind me! What if he'd caught me before I got to the car?" Her body began to tremble once again, but Dan was there to hold her in the safety and security of his arms. After she'd filled in her father-in-law on the details, he asked to speak to Dan.

"Dan? I don't know how we'll ever repay you. I thank God you were there. If anything had happened to our little Carlee—well, I'm not sure how Ethel and I could go on without her. Thanks, son!"

Dan blinked his eyes as another strange emotion flooded his soul. Jim had called him "son" again; his own father never called him that. He felt so close to Jim at that moment; it was as if they had a true kinship. "I don't know what it was, Jim. I couldn't sleep and felt compelled to go to the rink early this morning. Do you believe in people being psychic?"

Jim laughed. "I wouldn't call it psychic, Dan. I'd call it being led by God. I'm convinced He sent you to be there at just the right time, to keep Carlee from harm."

Dan hadn't considered it that way. The thought of God's leading frightened him, yet consoled him. More of those mixed emotions he'd been experiencing since meeting the Bennetts. "I told her I thought Santa should bring her a guard dog."

"Good idea! Been thinking that same thing myself. Maybe we ought to keep one around there on a full-time basis. Sure make me feel better about Carlee going in there by herself. I'll see what I can do about it."

When Dan hung up the phone, Carlee was waiting with their mugs of hot coffee. She was smiling, but Dan knew she was forcing a grin, trying to mask the fear that still surged through her body like ice water. He took the mugs and placed them on the counter, then wrapped her in his arms protectively. Funny, he'd been so concerned about protecting her, he hadn't been nervous or afraid for himself. He'd only wanted to get the guy that had terrified her so.

"What if you hadn't come early—do you think he would have followed me out the door? If he'd caught me, what—"

Dan put his big hand lightly over her mouth to keep her from finishing her sentence. "But he didn't! I *was* here. Jim said God sent me," he said reassuringly, surprising himself by his use of the word God.

She pressed her face into his chest as his arms encircled her body. "Oh, Dan. I praise the Lord that you were here."

The practice session was a total loss—his skating was erratic, his school figures lopsided. They decided to shut off the VCR and forget skating for the day. Their minds were too busy with what-ifs, although neither of them voiced them to the other.

"What time do you leave?" she asked as she slipped her hand into the crook of his arm. The fingers of his free hand gave her hand a gentle squeeze.

"Plane leaves in less than two hours. I should go pretty soon, I guess, but I don't want to leave." He lifted her fingers to his lips and kissed them tenderly as he looked into her wide eyes. "Why don't I call Brad and tell him I won't be there? I can't leave you here to open in the morning without me being here with you."

She lowered her head onto his shoulder as a smile curled her lips. "How do you think I've gotten along these past four years without you?"

He hadn't doubted that she'd gotten along without him— she was one of the strongest women he'd ever known. But somehow, he now felt responsible for her.

"Besides," she added confidently, "Father Bennett is going to come with me and check out the building the next two days while you're gone. I'll be fine. Just go and enjoy the wedding, and we'll see you on Wednesday."

It relieved his mind to know Jim Bennett would be with her. After all, he'd assured Brad he'd be at the wedding.

"Okay. But promise me that if Jim isn't with you, you won't open the door."

She promised, but both of them wondered what would happen when he left for good.

❧

Brad, Michelle, and a dozen other members of the cast of Ice Fantasy were waiting when Dan got off the plane in Tampa. They cheered and hugged one another, laughing and talking. Brad loaded Dan's things into his Porsche and suggested they all go for a beer. Everyone agreed, and they piled into their cars and headed for the nearest bar. The music was blaring when they entered—something about a brokenhearted cowboy whose woman had left him for another. Dan couldn't help but think it was probably the guy's singing that drove her away.

His old friend, Michelle, snuggled up next to Dan. He tried to move away but found it impossible with so many people crowded around the small table.

"Hey, honey! Beers all around and give me the tab!" Brad called to the waitress in a loud voice. When the beers were placed in front of them, Dan stared at his rather than drink it. Brad picked it up and shoved it into his hand. "You're the best man; aren't you going to toast the groom?"

When his friend put it that way, what choice did he have? Dan smiled his sheepish grin and lifted his glass. "Here's to Brad and Beth. May they have many happy years together." He turned to Brad, who was beaming with the attention. "And may their marriage last at least fifty years!"

The group fell silent. Brad rose to his feet and looked puzzled. "Come on, fella. I'm getting married—not facing a jail sentence. Fifty years with the same broad? Not me. We'll be lucky if we make it five. That's plenty!"

Dan frowned. "Then why are you getting married?"

"To make it legal, man. I figure five years and then I'm out and on to greener pastures. Too many fillies out there, and I'm a young man."

Dan placed his glass on the table. Get married with the idea of bailing out in five years? He and Brad had never seriously discussed marriage before. He'd had no idea his friend felt this way. "How does Beth feel about this, Brad?"

The group at the table looked from man to man, their heads bobbing as if they were watching a tennis match.

Brad shrugged his shoulders. "Fine with her! Look, Dan, we all know in this crazy business we're in there are lots of opportunities to cheat on your spouse. Just the groupies alone offer endless possibilities!" He aimed a knowing wink at his friends, who nodded their heads in agreement. "We've decided that if we find someone else we'd rather be with, it's over. We'll get a friendly divorce!" He raised his glass to the others, who were listening intently while they guzzled their beers. "In the meantime, we can file a joint tax return and save a few bucks. Everybody wins except the IRS."

The group cheered in unison and Dan felt sick. This is what he'd left Kansas City for?

"Hey, don't be a party pooper. Drink up! Have some fun!" It was Michelle, leaning on him, stroking his hair with her fingers. "Dance with me, Dan."

"Yeah," Brad agreed as he nudged Dan with his shoulder, "go dance with Michelle. You need to lighten up and enjoy yourself, buddy!"

Dan moved onto the dance floor with Michelle, then excused himself and left her standing in the middle of the floor. He had to get out of there; he felt that he was being smothered, that he didn't belong. He left.

For nearly two hours he leaned against Brad's car in the parking lot, waiting for a ride to the hotel. What was wrong with him? He loved parties! These were the people he partied with when they were on the road. They'd been in bars and clubs all over the world—Paris, London, Milan, Berlin, Singapore. What was so different about Florida?

Brad was a mess when he came teetering out of the bar; he was in no condition to drive. Dan tried to get his keys away from him, but Brad wouldn't give them up. Michelle was just as bad—after a few beers she thought she was Cleopatra. When Dan refused to get into the car with the two drunks, Brad sped off, squealing his tires as he left the crowded parking lot.

Dan stood there empty-handed; his luggage was in the trunk of Brad's car and he had no idea where Brad and Michelle were headed. He waited ten minutes, but they didn't return. Others from their group emerged and offered him a ride, but they were as soused as Brad and Michelle; he turned them down flat. They couldn't understand his reticence. He didn't understand it, either, but attributed it to his early morning episode with the burglar. Somehow it had made him see life for the fragile thing it was, and he didn't want to waste it with a bunch of inebriated people.

He called a cab, and once in the hotel, he phoned Carlee.

"How are things in Florida?"

He took a deep breath and lied. "Great! Spent some time with my friends. Talked about old times; had a blast."

"I'm glad for you," she said sincerely. "Are you all going out for dinner together?"

He glanced at his watch. "Yeah, in an hour or so. Going to a great place. What'd you and the kids have for supper?"

"You'd never guess. Roast beef sandwiches! Father Bennett sliced the rest of the roast into nice thin slices and brought some over to share with us."

Suddenly he had an insane desire for roast beef. "How are the kids? Did you tell them about this morning?"

"Most of it. They think you're a hero. So do I!"

"I'm no hero, Carlee." He was sure he could detect a twinge of fear as she spoke. "I miss you guys."

"Sure you do! With all those beautiful women surrounding you, you miss us? How gullible do you think I am, Dan?"

He knew she was teasing, but he wished he could convince her he was very serious. He did miss them.

"Where are you going to have the bachelor party?"

He straightened. The bachelor party! He'd forgotten all about it! He'd planned to invite the men in their circle of friends for an impromptu gathering at their favorite pub, then the beer guzzling took place and Brad had spun off with Michelle. He had no idea where to find him. What could he do? He didn't want Carlee to know what kind of people he hung around with. She'd trusted him with her children.

"Better go," he said while trying to mask his anxiety. "Bachelor party won't wait. Call you tomorrow." He sat down on the side of the bed. He needed a plan.

The phone rang. He picked it up, hoping it was Brad. But it wasn't. It was Beth and she was crying. "Speak slowly, Beth; I can't understand you. Tell me what's wrong."

The bride-to-be sniffled, took a few deep breaths, and began to explain the reason for her call. "I'm thinking of calling off the wedding, Dan, ending it with Brad. . ."

He struggled for words. "Why, Beth? I thought everything was fine between you two."

"That was *before* I got the phone call!" Now her voice sounded more angry than hurt.

"What phone call?"

"From the anonymous caller who told me I could find Brad at the Coconut Motel—with a woman."

Dan fidgeted with the phone cord. "You know better than to believe someone who won't give you a name. It was probably a prank, a prewedding joke."

"I want to think that, Dan. But to be honest, I don't trust Brad. This isn't the first time I've had doubts about him. I know he's no saint, but is any guy these days?"

"But—he told me you two had an agreement, something about walking away quietly if the other person ever decided he or she wanted out of the marriage."

"He told you that? That's bunk. He knows I don't feel that way. He's made that stupid statement in front of all our friends; I thought everyone knew he was kidding. *I* thought he was kidding!"

"So, what are you going to do?" Dan wanted to tell her about Brad and Michelle. Maybe the caller was right; maybe Brad *was* at the motel. But somehow he couldn't be the one to betray his old friend.

"Marry him, I guess. And hope the marriage will straighten him out. With all our family coming, it's probably too late to call it off, as much as I'd like to."

Dan placed the phone in its cradle and stared straight ahead. He'd only been away from these people for a week and a half; now he hardly knew them. They were like strangers.

He wanted to call Carlee again—tell her about Brad. And about Beth's call. He needed to hear her voice. But he couldn't. He tried Brad's apartment and got no answer.

A rap-rap sounded on his door at eight o'clock that evening. There stood Brad with bloodshot eyes, looking guilty, suitcase and garment bag in hand. "Hey, man. What can I say? I'm sorry."

Dan glared at his friend, and all he could think about was Beth's call. "Where have you been? With Michelle?"

Brad lowered his head and rubbed the toe of one shoe on the surface of the carpet. "Dropped her off at her place right after I left you."

Dan wanted to believe him but found it difficult in light of his discussion with Beth. "Honest, Brad?"

Brad looked Dan directly in the eye. "Honest."

"Guess you know you've messed up with your stupid antics. I'd wanted to have a bachelor party for you tonight—

get together with the guys—but you blew it. I had no idea how to find you. Where were you?"

"Driving around," he answered unconvincingly.

"In your condition? What'd you want to do? Kill yourself and maybe someone else? You were drunk, Brad."

Brad pushed past him and dropped onto the love seat in Dan's room. "Look, man. Tomorrow's my wedding day, so lighten up! What's the matter with you, anyway?"

"Did you spend the afternoon with Michelle, Brad?" He had to know.

Brad reddened and squared his jaw. "Dan, why would you ask me that? Of course not!"

Dan wanted to believe him, but how could he? "Brad, have you ever been to the Coconut Motel?"

Brad stiffened. "That roach motel? Why would you ask?" He behaved as if he were offended that Dan would even ask.

Dan hoped his friend's response had been the sign of true indignation and decided to let the subject drop. "Never mind. How about dinner? My treat!" He grabbed the soon-to-be groom by the arm and ushered him out of the room. "Now, what do you want for your last dinner as a free man?"

ten

It was Tuesday morning. Carlee woke at 4:45 and thought of Dan. He'd probably be sleeping still, exhausted from his bout with the burglar, the flight to Florida, and the bachelor party. She found herself wishing he hadn't gone to Florida. Had he left only yesterday? It seemed like it had been a week. She'd known Dan for such a short time; how could she miss him this much? She'd understood from the beginning that he'd be in Kansas City for three weeks and then he'd disappear from her life—probably forever. She'd been so careful to keep an impenetrable shell around her life. Yet Dan had worked his way into it without even trying. And without intending to, she'd welcomed and encouraged him.

❧

Dan Castleberry was wide awake at 4:45 and wondering if Jim Bennett had remembered to set his alarm clock. The last thing he wanted was to have Carlee entering that building alone. Carlee. Hard to believe that less than two weeks ago, he hadn't even known she existed. Yet here he was, worrying about her. If Jim didn't get her a dog, he was going to. No woman should be out alone that time of morning. And to think that she'd been doing it for four years. But it was obvious she'd do anything for those kids of hers. He'd wanted to tell Brad about Carlee. She'd been on his mind throughout dinner. But what could he tell him? That he'd made friends with a young widow and her two small children? That the times he'd been in her home were some of the happiest times he'd ever had? That he'd spent big bucks for a doll? For two of them? And an autographed baseball? That he could hardly wait to get back to Kansas City to

92

see her again and hold her in his arms? No. Brad wouldn't understand, never in a million years. Brad had known how important his career was to him, how focused his life had been. No, this was not the time to discuss Carlee.

Tom Cord, Ice Fantasy's administrator, phoned an hour later and, after the usual greeting, invited Dan to come to company headquarters at around ten. When Dan entered the office, Tom welcomed him, shook his hand, and motioned him toward a chair; then he eyed him intently. "We've got a problem, Dan. With twelve cast members. I know they're your friends, but they've been hitting the bottle pretty hard." He moved around his desk, dropped into the comfortable leather chair, and steepled his fingers. "I don't know if it was because you stayed behind in Kansas City and he missed your influence or what, but Brad joined in big-time, and he's been on one big drunk since he arrived here." Tom Cord frowned as he closed his eyes and pressed back in his chair. "Dan, I know you haven't been a part of this mess; I've never even seen you the least bit tipsy. I've been watching this situation for some time now, and believe me, I'm not happy about it."

Dan slumped in his chair. He'd been afraid something like this was happening, but he'd tried to ignore it.

Tom continued. "I've warned the whole lot of them that if they don't straighten up, I'm going to have to replace them."

"But—"

"I can't have this, Dan. Ice Fantasy is a family show. We have a reputation to maintain. And I need people who are dependable. Not a bunch of drunks!"

Dan felt sick. "What can I do?"

Tom walked around his desk and stood facing his friend, a troubled furrow on his brow. "I honestly don't know, Dan. Brad is jeopardizing his career. I hope his marriage to Beth will be the answer; she's got a fairly level head."

Dan ran his tongue over suddenly dry lips. "I feel responsible.

I was so caught up in my own life, I never even noticed how out of control he's gotten."

"He's a big boy, Dan. He's brought this on himself." Tom breathed a deep sigh. "Business is business. I hate to be the bearer of bad tidings, but I thought you should know. You being his best friend. Maybe you can talk to him." He placed a heavy hand on Dan's shoulder. "If he'll listen to anyone, I think it'll be you. He respects you."

Dan stood and extended his hand. "I'll do what I can, Tom. Thanks for clueing me in."

He took a cab to the hotel and scaled the steps to his room. The wedding wasn't until seven; he'd have plenty of time to call Carlee. He needed to hear her voice. The line was busy when he placed the call. He ordered room-service coffee, stretched out on the bed, and thought about his future. His long-range plans were right on target. He wasn't about to mess up like Brad and the others—he'd worked too hard, too long, to throw it all away foolishly. He smiled as he thought about Carlee. He missed being with her and the children, but skating was his life. And although he'd enjoyed being with her. . .

Suddenly he realized he wasn't being honest with himself. Carlee was much more than a friend! He'd devoted a third of his life to his career, but was it enough? Could he be passing up the love of a lifetime by walking away from Carlee Bennett? Could God actually have sent him to the Ice Palace like Jim said? He dialed again and waited. She answered on the first ring.

"Oh, Dan. I'm so glad to hear your voice. I've been think-ing about you. How did the bachelor party go?"

He paused, wondering how much he should tell her and decided to come clean and tell her everything, including the part about Brad, Michelle, and Beth's phone call.

"Oh, Dan, I'm sorry. You two were such good friends."

"Well, not much I can do about it. I'm going to talk to him

if I get a chance. But I want to hear about you. Did Jim go with you to the rink this morning?"

"Yes. But, Dan, he's not going to be able to do that every morning. It's too much for him—his schedule is so full. I told him that once you were gone, I'd see about getting a dog."

Dan stifled a laugh. "Are you saying I can be replaced by a dog?"

She giggled. "Oh, Dan, of course not. Father Bennett said he could take the dog home with him at night, and I could bring him back to the rink with me. What do you think?"

He breathed a sigh; at least she'd have some protection. "Sounds like a good idea to me."

"What time are you coming home tomorrow? The children and I will pick you up at the airport."

"Thanks. You sure you're up to it? The airport will be crowded."

"Couldn't keep us away."

At 5:30, Dan donned his tuxedo and took a cab to the church, where he was to meet Brad. It was a beautiful evening. It occurred to him that he should have invited Carlee and the kids to come along with him; he could have stayed on a few days longer and taken them to Disney World. Whoa! Back up! What was he thinking? How had that idea entered his head? Take kids to Disney World? This was Dan Castleberry, world-renowned skater. Confirmed bachelor. His mind must be slipping.

The chapel where the wedding was to be held was small and crowded. As Dan stood next to the groom, he hoped Brad had told the truth about Michelle and the motel, but the look on Brad's face when Michelle entered the chapel said otherwise.

All eyes turned to the double doors at the back of the church as the strains of "Here Comes the Bride" filled the room and Beth entered, dressed in a flowing gown of white satin and lace. That is, all eyes except Brad's. His eyes zeroed in on Michelle first, then flitted toward his bride. Only Dan noticed his distraction—no one else. Not even Beth; she was too happy, too caught up in wedding joys to notice. Dan wanted to shout out, to stop the wedding, but he didn't. Instead he stood by, helplessly silent. When he heard the words, "If any person has just cause why these two should not be united in holy matrimony, may he speak now or forever hold his peace," his heart pounded violently in his chest. He reminded himself that he didn't actually know the truth. Brad had denied he'd spent the afternoon with Michelle in the motel. Who was he to accuse his friend? He watched as the newly wedded couple strode down the aisle. Mr. and Mrs. Brad Morris, the seemingly perfect couple. The wedding was over. All Dan could do now was hope for the best. The duplicity he'd witnessed sickened him.

He phoned Carlee the minute he got back to his room. A young boy answered. "Bennett residence. Bobby speaking."

Dan smiled when he heard the child's voice. "And how are you, Mr. Bennett? Are you taking good care of your mother and sister while I'm away?"

"Hi, Dan! When are you coming home?"

The word "home" made Dan sad. Home was wherever he was at the time. It wasn't Kansas City, where his parents lived. Or Florida, where Ice Fantasy was headquartered. He didn't have a home, not a real one. His home was a suitcase packed with his personal belongings. Home was somewhere off in the future when he would retire from the ice show and settle down.

"Tomorrow, Bobby. I'll be landing in Kansas City at seven P.M. And I'm really anxious to see you and Becca."

"Great! Mama said we could pick you up in the minivan. Becca wants to talk to you, okay?"

He smiled as visions of Becca sitting on his lap listening to his distorted fairy tales filled his thoughts.

"When ya comin' home, Dan? I miss you."

"Tomorrow, Becca. Tomorrow. And I miss you, too. Now let me talk to your mother. Okay, honey?"

"I love you, Dan," the tiny voice answered.

Carlee's voice could be heard in the background as she instructed the children to get ready for bed. Then, "Hi, Dan. We've been waiting for your call. You wouldn't believe these kids; they wouldn't go to bed until we heard from you. How did the wedding go?"

He gave her a run-through of the day's happenings, including the eye-contact episode between Brad and Michelle.

"You shouldn't feel responsible, Dan. He made his decisions himself. You couldn't have changed his mind even if you'd known about Michelle. We'll have to pray that his improprieties are a thing of the past, that he and Beth will have a wonderful, long-lasting marriage."

How like her, he thought, *always willing to give the benefit of the doubt to any person.* "Think prayer will be enough? It'll take a miracle to keep those two together."

"That's what prayers for, Dan. Miracles do happen!"

Dan had never prayed before coming into contact with the Bennetts. But now he welcomed it, as long as he wasn't the one who had to do it. "Hey, what am I doing, burdening you with all of this? You don't even know these people," he said apologetically. "The main reason I called, other than to hear your voice, was to tell you I'd be arriving at KCI at seven tomorrow night—if the offer to pick me up still stands."

"You bet it does. If you're sure it won't embarrass you if two eager kids come along; they refuse to be left behind."

The hotel room suddenly seemed cold and impersonal; he could hardly wait to leave it. "Thanksgiving still on?"

"Last time I looked at the calendar, Thanksgiving was still scheduled for Thursday," she teased. The warmth of her laughter seemed to beckon him to Kansas City.

eleven

At exactly seven o'clock, Dan rushed through the walkway into the airport and was greeted by three smiling faces. He shook hands with Bobby, grabbed Becca up in his arms, and hugged Carlee. He was back in Kansas City and glad to be there. The trip to Florida had been stressful and exhausting.

The house smelled of pumpkin pie when they entered. Dan rushed into the kitchen and found two pies resting on the counter on cooling racks. "Just one slice?" he begged as he touched a fingertip to the top of one of the spicy pies.

"No," Becca said firmly as she tugged on his hand. "Mama said we gotta wait 'til tomorrow!"

Carlee smiled. "Dan is here now, children, and it's past your bedtime. I want both of you in your pajamas. Pronto!"

Two unhappy children obediently followed their mother's command, kissed Dan, and headed for their bedrooms.

She grinned at Dan. "*Now* you can have some pie!"

It was the best pie he'd ever eaten. And he told her so.

She beamed with pride at his generous comments.

Tomorrow he would experience the first home-cooked Thanksgiving meal he'd eaten since his grandmother died. His memories of his grandmother may have faded slightly, but he remembered her well. Yes, tomorrow would be Thanksgiving, and there'd be more pumpkin pie.

❧

Long, ragged bands of red and pink laced across the horizon and pierced the gray-blue early morning sky as the sun began to peek through the leafless trees. It was Thanksgiving morning, and Carlee was up and out of bed to greet its arrival. But this morning, unlike most, she would be heading to her kitchen, not the Ice Palace.

As she sat on the edge of the bed tying her tennies, she caught sight of the wedding picture that had remained on her nightstand these four years since Robert was so quickly taken from her. She lifted the gold-framed photograph and hugged it to her breast. Memories of other Thanksgivings flooded her mind and her heart. Robert had been the nearly perfect husband; they'd been so happy. Why had God allowed him to die? She'd asked that question a thousand times. So had the Bennetts, but no answer had come. Yet in its place had come a peace, an assurance that God was in control. Reddened eyes stared back at her as she gazed into the mirror. Today was a special day; a dinner guest was coming.

ð

Dan Castleberry woke at sunrise, raised up on one elbow, and peered out the east window of his room. There was something he loved about a sunrise, and this one was a doozie. Long red-and-pink bands were spread across the horizon as though a painter were testing the colors of his palette, splashing them boldly across the canvas. Tossing back the covers, he stepped to the window and watched with wonder as the new day spilled out before him in all its splendor—clean, fresh, and new. He would spend the day with Carlee, Bobby, and Becca, a real family Thanksgiving.

There was no aroma of turkey roasting in the oven, no pies lining the kitchen counter, no cranberry salad chilling in the refrigerator at his parents' house. They didn't have a clue what Thanksgiving was all about. But did he? Had any previous Thanksgivings been meaningful to him? Where had he spent them? In cities where he hadn't known a soul, in restaurants too numerous to remember, with people he cared little about.

Suddenly, without announcement or fanfare, the sun's rays

broke over the trees and filled his world with light. The darkness of both his thoughts and the night were banished by the
arrival of a new day, brilliant and warm. A day full of
promise and hope. Dan felt an inner joy. Today would be
special; Carlee and the children would have a real family
Thanksgiving, and he would be part of it.

&.

By ten o'clock the scent of roasting turkey and sage dressing
filled the Bennett house. The salads were chilled, the corn
casserole was ready to pop into the oven, the homemade
Parkerhouse rolls were rising; dinner was well under control.
Bobby and Becca were watching an Odyssey videotape, and
Carlee was putting the finishing touches on the cheesecake.
The sound of the Gaither Vocal Band filled the kitchen, and
her spirits soared as she harmonized along with them. Dan
was due at eleven and life was good. On a whim, she crossed
the room and dialed his number. He answered almost immediately. "Aha! You're sitting on the phone. Who did you think
would call, Ed McMahon or Dick Clark?"

"Naw, what would I do with ten million smackeroos?
What's up?"

She felt a little foolish calling him; her mother had always
cautioned that girls shouldn't call boys for no good reason.
Funny she should think of that now. But Dan was hardly a
boy. And she was way beyond the girl stage. Friends should
be able to call friends, shouldn't they? "I was thinking about
you, wondering if you were busy? I thought maybe you'd
like to come over a little early."

"Sure, if you need help." His voice sounded eager.

She laughed into the phone. "You? Help in the kitchen?
That's hard to imagine! I'll probably just have you sit on the
stool and lick spoons. But I would enjoy your company."

"Tell the kids I'm on my way. Should I pick up anything?
Bread? Whipping cream? Peanuts?"

"Just bring yourself; you're all we need."

Dan arrived fifteen minutes later and found two eager children waiting on the porch for him. Bobby ran to Dan's car with Becca three steps behind. The man stooped, grabbed a child in each arm, and swung them about in big circles before depositing them on the front porch.

He'd been so busy with the kids that he hadn't noticed the lovely young woman standing just inside the storm door, watching the scene with a satisfied smile. When he finally caught sight of her, he was sure he felt his heart skip a beat. She wore a soft white blouse and an ankle-length calico jumper, topped with a freshly starched red apron. He thought she looked like a page plucked from an *Ideals* magazine. He couldn't take his eyes off her.

Becca and Bobby held his hands and dragged him into the house while their mother held the door open for them.

"Dan, I'm so glad you're here," she said as she helped him remove his jacket and hung it in the hall closet.

"I'm glad I'm here, too," he stammered awkwardly, wondering why all of a sudden he found it difficult to express himself. What he really wanted to do was pull her into his arms and smother her with kisses.

Bobby and Becca tugged at his hands and pulled him toward the family room.

"No!" their mother said firmly. "There will be plenty of time for that later. I invited Dan over early to help me; he has work to do. You two go watch your video and leave him alone. This morning he's all mine. Now, obey me."

The two children dropped their hold on his hands and did as told. He watched, grinning, as they walked away. "They're good kids. I love being with them; you know that."

"I know. But for now, like I said, you're all mine. They'll have to wait their turn." She took his hand in hers and, with a sideways glance that melted his heart, pulled him into the kitchen and tied an apron about his waist. "Here," she ordered as she extended her open palm, which held a paring knife and a potato peeler. "Choose your weapon."

He considered the choices and selected the peeler. She pointed to a five-pound sack of potatoes waiting on the kitchen table. "Peel!"

Dan peeled potatoes while Carlee mixed the homemade garlic dressing and tossed the green salad. He hoped she wouldn't catch him gazing at her as he peeled away at the sink. This was all so new to him, watching a woman working in her kitchen and enjoying it. He'd always thought women hated this sort of thing. Wasn't that why take-out food and restaurants were such an important part of the American culture? Wouldn't it have been easier to eat out, as his parents would? Yet here she was, working away and apparently loving it. Would he ever understand Carlee Bennett? He'd never been around another woman like her.

With the potatoes simmering in the big glass pot in the microwave, Carlee showed Dan where the silverware was kept and began to set the table with her best china. The two stood back to admire their handiwork when they finished.

"I've never set a table before," Dan admitted as he adjusted one of the spoons he'd placed a little haphazardly.

She patted him on the arm. "Well, you did an admirable job, Mr. Castleberry—for a first-timer. I'm proud of you."

Funny. He'd received the applause and accolades of audiences all over the world for his skating ability, but this one small compliment from Carlee was every bit as important to him. He liked having her approval for the things he did. He liked everything about her.

"I'm gonna put that big pat of butter in the middle like Ethel did," Dan declared as he mashed the potatoes while Carlee stirred the gravy. "Umm, that was good."

The children placed the butter, salt and pepper, and relish

tray on the table while Dan carried in the turkey on the big oval platter. "Where do you want this bird?" he asked as he eyed the golden-brown treasure.

"At your place—at the head of the table," she answered with an impish grin. "You're going to carve."

Dan's eyes widened. "Me? Carve? I don't know how."

"The bird doesn't know the difference, and we won't tell. Will we, kids?" She and the two children snickered at his chagrin. "Here's the electric carving knife," she invited as she extended it toward him. "Have at it!"

Once the table was laden with all the Thanksgiving delicacies, Carlee directed everyone to their chairs. Dan was at the head of the table with Carlee opposite him, and a child sat on either side. Dan knew what was coming and took a child's hand in each of his own, while Carlee did the same, completing the circle. He hoped she wouldn't ask him to pray; he'd been worrying about that ever since she'd invited him. Praying aloud was not in his bag of tricks!

She gave him an understanding glance. "I'll say grace today." When she finished praying and they'd all joined in for the "amen," Carlee smiled at her guest and said with a smile, "Let's eat. Dan, pass the turkey!"

He picked up the platter loaded with juicy slices of turkey, carved in ways no turkey had ever been carved before, and grinned. "Kinda mangled him, didn't I?"

"I think it's purty, Dan." Becca pulled a long, slender wedge of white meat from the platter and stuffed it into her tiny mouth.

"Becca, please!" Her mother grabbed a napkin and dabbed at the little girl's mouth. "Where are your manners?"

"Dan did it in the kitchen; I saw him," Becca accused as she chomped on the juicy turkey breast. They all laughed as the turkey began its trip around the table.

Dan took big helpings from each dish and platter as it

passed by: steaming mashed potatoes smothered with melted butter; rich brown gravy; creamy corn casserole; sweet potatoes laden with brown sugar and melted marshmallows; hot, melt-in-your-mouth Parkerhouse rolls; thick red cranberry sauce; all the wonderful salads; and of course, thick slices of tender turkey. Carlee watched with a look of satisfaction as Dan consumed mountains of food. It'd been a long time since she'd cooked for a man, other than Father Bennett. Dan's enjoyment made it all worthwhile.

He took the final bite of a buttered roll, sipped the last of the coffee in his cup, leaned back in his chair, and smiled at his hostess. "Carlee, this is the best meal I've had in my entire life! How can I ever thank you?"

She returned his smile. "By helping me clear the table and load the dishwasher, that's how." Dan stood and began scraping and stacking the dishes, eager to do his part as an appreciative guest.

"Dan!" she pled as she rushed around the table and grabbed him by the arm, "I was kidding—stop! Go on into the family room with the children and read the paper—or take a nap. I'll clean up in here."

He caught her by the hand. "Mrs. Bennett, you've spent no-telling how many hours preparing this delicious meal for the children and me, and now you expect to clean up after us while I read the paper or take a nap? No way! I'm in this thing to the end. It's only fair. Let's get at it."

For seconds their eyes locked. It was nice to share the good and the bad with someone. He had no one and she'd lost Robert. Certainly, on this day, they could help one another.

The two worked as a team, scraping, wiping, cleaning, putting away, and loading until the kitchen was immaculate. She untied Dan's apron, then turned her back to him so he could untie hers. He kissed her lightly on top of her head, nestling his face in her hair. This time, without hesitation, she responded to his touch, turning and wrapping her arms about his neck. He bent and kissed first one eyelid, then the other. His lips brushed both of her cheeks as she leaned into him. He wanted to hold her forever, to never let her go. What was happening to him?

They parted, and without a word, Dan took her hand and led her slowly into the family room where the children were playing quietly on the floor. He pulled her onto the couch beside him, enveloped her in his arms, and there they sat, full and satisfied. Thanksgiving had been a success; all but the dessert had been devoured, and it would come later.

"One more week," Dan said under his breath.

"What?"

He tightened his arm and pulled her closer to him. "One more week and I'll be gone."

She pursed her lips and frowned. "I know."

"I'll miss you—and the children."

"I hope so; we'll miss you."

He cupped her chin with his hand and lifted her face to his. "Carlee Bennett. You've been a confusing influence on my life; do you know that?"

Her eyes searched his. "What do you mean?"

"I thought I had life pretty well figured out. Then I came here and met you and your family. Now I don't understand life at all." His lips brushed her forehead lightly. "Somehow, the life I'd worked so hard to achieve seems pretty empty now. I didn't realize how true that is until I went to Florida for the wedding."

She sat straight up and turned to face him directly. "But you're the star of Ice Fantasy! You're able to travel the world, see new places, meet new people. And probably draw a good salary to boot. How could our routine little lives have you confused?" She spoke as though she were the one who was confused.

He pulled her back into the cradle of his arm and tightened his grip. "I can't explain it to myself, let alone someone else. I don't understand what's happened to me."

She lifted her face and met his eyes. "Is it because of your friend Brad? He's made you second-guess your life?"

He paused and traced her eyebrows with his fingertip. "May have something to do with it. I'm sure his marriage will be nothing like what you and Robert had. I want a love like that, Carlee. Like yours and Robert's."

A little voice broke into their conversation. "I want some pie!" Becca clamored as she climbed onto Dan's lap.

"Okay. Okay. Why don't I help your mother, and if we're good, maybe she'll let us bring it in here and we kids can eat it on the coffee table. What do you say to that, Mama?" he pleaded on behalf of an endearing little girl and her brother.

Carlee cocked her head and frowned as if considering the offer. "You kids drive a hard bargain." She extended her hand to Dan, who took it gratefully, and the two walked arm in arm into the kitchen where the dessert waited to be served. "Okay, but ya gotta watch the crumbs!"

twelve

The family and Dan shared a wonderful, leisurely afternoon together. After a late supper of leftovers, followed by a bedtime story, Carlee put the children to bed while Dan read the newspaper. Then he devoured the last sliver of pumpkin pie. "Umm, that pie could've won a blue ribbon!" he mumbled as he rubbed his tummy and pushed back in the recliner.

"With or without the huge dollop of whipped cream you put on it?" Carlee teased as she watched him relax in the chair.

He linked his fingers behind his head and closed his eyes. "Secret recipe? One of Mother Bennett's?"

"Off the Libby's pumpkin can," she replied with a giggle.

He opened his eyes wide. "Are you serious?"

"Dead serious," she said with a twisted smile as she lifted his empty dish and fork from the end table. When she came back from the kitchen, she found him sleeping contentedly in the chair. She kissed him softly on the cheek and settled herself into the corner of the sofa with her book.

A half hour later Dan opened his eyes. He looked around and rubbed his eyes vigorously. "What time is it?"

"Eight-thirty, sleepyhead. You've had quite a nap."

He rotated his shoulders. "Why didn't you wake me up?"

"You looked so cute, just like a little boy. I couldn't bring myself to disturb you."

"Tell me; did I drool?" he asked as he sat up straight and rubbed at the stubble on his chin.

"No. But you did snore a bit." She diverted her eyes and smothered her desire to laugh aloud.

He lowered the footrest on the chair, leaned forward, and looked embarrassed. "Did I really?"

She faked a frown. "Sounded like a grizzly bear."

He crossed the room to the sofa and lowered himself onto the cushion beside her, then slipped his arm around her shoulders. "You wouldn't kid me, would you?"

"Now, would I do that?" she asked with a coy smile.

He grinned, then stood and extended his hand and pulled her to her feet. "I've had a wonderful day with you and the kids; I can't thank you enough for inviting me. And to think you prepared all that delicious food yourself. Well, I'm impressed, to say the least."

She looped her arms about his neck. "Dan, I wanted you to come spend the day with us. I love having you here. You've filled a void in my life—a big empty hole left by Robert." Fearing she wasn't making herself clear, she looked into his dark eyes and continued. "Not in the same way, of course. I loved him deeply. I never expected to find that kind of love again. Oh, I've put on a good front. No one, not even the Bennetts, know how lonely I've been." She brushed a lock of hair from his forehead. "I wasn't looking for a husband, Dan. Does that make sense? Can you understand what I'm saying?"

He tilted her chin upward toward his. "Sure, I understand. I feel the same way. I was pretty lonely, too."

She leaned her head on his chest and rested it there, enjoying his scent and the strength of his masculinity.

His chin rested on her brow. "Then I met Carlee and her children. My life changed. You've opened your home and your hearts to me and I've felt—well, important. At times, even needed. I like that feeling. It's going to be hard to leave you. I could get used to your way of life pretty easily."

Things were progressing far beyond their self-imposed limits. Dan would be leaving soon; they'd each vowed to themselves that they wouldn't get entangled like this. "You'd better be going. You've got practicing to do in the morning, remember?" she whispered. She didn't want him to leave, but it was getting late, and she could feel her resolve weakening. She'd have to let him go when his time was up in Kansas City; she might as well get used to it now. There was no future for them together. To think otherwise would be inviting heartbreak.

He dropped his arms and backed off slowly. "Umm. . . okay. You're right. See you in the morning. And don't forget: You are not—I repeat, not—to get out of your car if you get there before I do. Promise?"

She smiled. "I promise."

He watched as she pulled his jacket from the closet. She looked like a little girl in the calico pinafore, not the strong, independent woman he knew her to be, and he wanted to hold her. To protect her. The thought of her being trapped in the rink with the man he'd captured made his blood run cold. He couldn't let that happen again. But, how could he prevent it? In a few days he'd be miles away.

She held his jacket as he slipped his arms into the sleeves, then walked him to the door, where Dan held her close and they said their good-byes.

He leaned against the storm door after it closed behind him. Getting involved with the young widow and her children would ruin the master plan he'd laid out for his life. And it would mean getting involved with God. He wasn't ready for that, or ready to give up his career. But. . .

❧

When she pulled her minivan into the lot at 5:15 the next morning, Dan was sitting in his car waiting for her. He insisted that she stay in her locked van until he'd opened and checked out the building.

After their wake-up coffee, he moved onto the ice and skated the entire hour without stopping. "Good practice. Felt good to get my skates on again."

"Uh-huh." She pulled her collar up and shivered.

He wrapped his arms around her and held her close. "That better? I get so warm skating, I forget how cold it is in here for you. You're not taking cold, are you?"

"No. I'm fine, Dan. I could've gone into the lobby where it's a little warmer, but I like watching you. You're a wonderful skater. I'm sure I'm the envy of the Kansas City skating crowd, being an audience-of-one to watch the famous Dan Castleberry skate. Do you think I'd let a cold building stop me? I'm no pansy, you know."

The buzzer sounded and she was off to open the door for the patchers and their mothers. Dan put his skates into the office and left, saying he'd phone later.

Carlee was able to finish her bookwork in record time and wandered into the rink area to watch the patchers. After the last ones had shut the door behind them, she checked her watch and discovered she had more than a half hour to kill before the employees would arrive and she'd have to open the door. On sudden impulse, she ran to her office and pulled her figure skates from the closet shelf. It'd been months since she'd skated—entirely too long. She needed the exercise.

She moved through the doors, slipped off the protective rockers, and glided smoothly onto the ice with long, even strokes. It felt good, relaxing. Before long, she was moving rapidly across the surface, turning first one way and then the other, whirling and twirling comfortably. As she rounded the end of the rink, she caught sight of a face peering through the lobby window. It was Dan! He'd been watching her skate. When he realized she'd spotted him, he stepped through the doors and walked onto the ice to join her. She knew she was in for it now—her secret was out.

"Carlee! Why didn't you tell me you were a skater?"

She giggled, embarrassed yet pleased at his reaction to her hidden talent. He took her hands in his and held them tightly.

"Tomorrow morning, Carlee Bennett. *You* are going to skate with me. And, I won't take no for an answer!"

"But—"

"But nothing! You did say you'd do whatever you could to help me, didn't you?"

She stood there, without excuse. "I. . .I guess I. . .said that."

"I needed to practice those pair numbers, but it's been close to impossible without a partner. Now I have one. You!"

"Dan! I couldn't!" she protested as she backed away. "Skate with Dan Castleberry, the star skater? Never!"

He pulled her close once again. "Oh, yes, you will. I've been watching you for some time, Carlee. I know what you can do, and I'm counting on you to help me," he explained as he released her hands and moved off the ice. "Oh, and thanks for giving me a key to the building; I would have missed your performance if I hadn't had a key. Tomorrow, Carlee!"

ૐ

Carlee didn't see Dan the rest of the day, but he called her that evening. "Whatcha been doing?" he asked.

Her spirits perked up at the sound of his voice and she relaxed. For some reason, the kids had driven her up the wall all afternoon with their magpie chattering. "Just put the kids to bed and fixed myself a cup of cocoa."

"Umm. With marshmallows?"

"Uh-huh, marshmallows. The big ones. What have you been doing today?" she queried as she took a sip of the rich drink.

Dan shuffled the charts on his lap. "Been going over the diagrams of the pair numbers so you can help me with them in the morning. You're gonna skate with me, remember?"

That very thought had haunted her all day. "How could I forget? I've been trying to come up with some reason, short of breaking a leg, to turn you down. You've got to promise you won't laugh. Or ask too much of me," she cautioned as she spooned out a marshmallow and popped it into her mouth.

"Forget it! You're committed. I don't expect you to do any of the fancy stuff, I just need you to skate the basic fundamentals of the routine. I'll be gentle; I promise." He asked about Bobby and Becca, and Jim and Ethel, then brought the conversation around to the true purpose of his call. "Carlee, you told me Bobby would be out of school Monday afternoon because of a teachers' meeting. I heard of a pretty little lake not far from here, near Lawrence. I thought we could go on a picnic, just the four of us. What do you say?"

She pondered his question. "Sure; sounds fine to me. The kids'll be excited; they love picnics."

"Not half as excited as the guy who invited them," he confessed in a half-whisper. "See you in the morning.

☙

Her body was chilled to the bone as she sat in the rink clutching her figure skates. It wasn't the temperature that caused the chill—it was the thought of skating with the star skater.

Dan left the ice and walked toward her, his hands in his pockets. "Ready?" He knelt as he began to loosen the laces on one of her skate boots.

"Not really. I don't think I—"

"Hush and give me your foot," he said firmly.

"But. . .you don't have to. . . ," she protested as she slid her feet back under the chair's rung, away from his grasp.

He held out his hand, palm up. "Oh, but I want to, Mrs. Bennett. Remember, you're dealing with Prince Charming. Snow White allowed him to put the shoe on her foot."

"That was Cinderella, you goof!" she stated with a muffled giggle as she extended her foot.

"Oh, yeah?" Dan laughed aloud with an impish grin. "Wrong fairy tale! I've been a prince so many times, I sometimes get my heroines mixed up. Sorry!" He placed the blade of her skate on his knee and began to draw the laces up snugly about her foot and ankle.

Carlee sat silently and watched him work. She wondered why God had allowed this man into her life. She could so easily fall in love with him. His gentleness, his concern for her welfare, his attachment to her children—everything she could want in a man. Well, almost everything. Two major things separated them. *Oh, well,* she reminded herself. *Be grateful for small favors. Having Dan in our lives for three weeks was better than no Dan at all.*

"Lovely lady, may I have this dance?" He extended his hand with a winsome smile as he motioned toward the ice.

"Sure. I guess," she stammered with uncertainty as she took his hand and rose to feet that seemed brittle and clumsy beneath her.

They stepped in unison onto the ice. Dan bent his arm and tucked her fingers into the crook of his arm, and they moved off, side by side, with long, steady strokes. After several revolutions around the rink, she began to relax and enjoy it.

"I have a feeling you've waltzed on skates before, right?" Without waiting for an answer, he did a quick three-turn in front of her and looped his arm about her waist, and they moved into a dance position. "Get ready now. . . ," he directed. "One, two, three, and glide."

"The Blue Danube"—one of her favorites. She started to hum softly as she and Dan whirled in long, slow circles about the glossy surface. It felt wonderful, like she was floating. With his firm arms guiding her, all she had to do was follow his lead.

When the music ended they stopped waltzing, but he continued to hold her fast, his arm about her waist, her hand in his. For a moment, she felt dizzy. Not from the twisting and turning, but from the emotions that whirled in her head and heart, and she cautioned herself, *Get with it, Carlee. With him, this is business; you're only a prop!*

Dan lowered his face and buried it in her hair. "Now, was that so bad?" he whispered as his lips brushed hers.

She leaned against him slowly, her forehead touching his freshly shaven chin. "No. Actually, it was pretty nice."

"Carlee. . .woman of a thousand surprises." He planted a lingering kiss on her temple before easing his hold on her. What was happening? Why was he drawn to this woman, this mother of two? He was Dan Castleberry, a man at the pinnacle of his profession, a world traveler. He could have any woman he wanted. Groupies flocked to him, literally throwing themselves at his feet. This whole Kansas City thing with the Bennetts didn't make any sense. They had become the center of his life since he'd arrived; he rarely even thought of his friends in Florida. He stepped away from her, as if to force a separation between the two of them, and rubbed his hands together briskly. "I'd say you're a natural skater. Are you sure you wouldn't like to give this all up and run away with me and join Ice Fantasy?" he joked as they headed toward the coffeepot, arm in arm.

"Yeah," she chided with a nudge of her elbow. "Think they'd want my kids, too? I could furnish my own dwarfs!"

"Carlee, thanks," he said sincerely as they walked through the double doors leading to the lobby. "Honest. You don't know how it's going to help to have you skate these numbers with me. I know you didn't really want to skate with me, and if you'd rather not continue, I'll understand."

A timid smile curled her lips as she looked into his face. "How could I refuse? Of course I'll do it. That is, unless you're only trying to make me feel good and really don't want me to skate with you." She tapped his chin with her fingertip. "I'm a big girl. I won't cry if you tell me my skating stinks!"

He swung around and grabbed her up in a big bear hug. "Carlee Bennett, I can't think of another woman on this planet I'd rather skate with than you."

She lifted her face and peeked over his arm. "Good. 'Cause right now, I'm your only choice."

He gave her another quick squeeze before turning her loose. "Settled. Case closed." His boyish smile suddenly turned into a frown. "I just remembered I promised my dad I'd play golf with him and a couple of his cronies today. At the speed they play, it'll take all day. I'd hoped to spend some time with the kids today; since Bobby is out of school, I'd planned to help him with his skating."

She patted his cheek. "I'm disappointed, too. Becca and Bobby had expected to see you today."

A hint of a smile began to form on his face. "You could invite me over for supper. They'll be done playing golf by then—unless they play by flashlight!"

"I might be persuaded to round up a pot of chili," she volunteered as she smoothed out a fold in his shirt collar.

His eyes penetrated hers. Having someone concerned about something as insignificant as a wrinkle was a new experience for him. And he found he liked it. No, he reveled in it. "I'd be mighty grateful, little lady. I've had a hankerin' for chili ever since I came in off the trail. And so has my horse!"

"Surely not John Wayne!" His impression lacked authenticity but she appeared to be amused by it anyway, and she laughed, something she did often since Dan had first come to her door that cold morning.

"Nope! Clint Eastwood!" he cajoled as he lifted one eyebrow and cocked his head. "Couldn't you tell?"

⁂

Dan arrived promptly at six P.M. Two scrubbed and combed children tussled all the way to the door to see who would get there first to open it for him.

"Dan! Dan!" little Becca screamed in her high-pitched baby voice as Dan scooped her up and hugged her to his chest.

Bobby wrapped his skinny arms about Dan's waist and held on tight. "Hi, Dan," the boy said as he ducked back and forth, trying to avoid his sister's swinging feet.

Dan reached down with his free arm and wrapped it around Bobby, pulling the youngster against him. "Hi, Bobby. I've missed you!"

The little boy seemed to melt into Dan's body as he pressed close to the man, his arms entwined with the skater's legs.

The familiar lump rose in Carlee's throat. Just one week and it'd all be over. "Hi, Dan," she said softly, not wanting to take anything away from her children's welcome.

He stood there looking at her as if he wanted to lock this moment in his memory. "Hi, Carlee. Thanks for letting me come," he said almost sadly.

She wondered if he was thinking the same thing she was, if he was counting down the days. Could this time they'd had together possibly mean as much to him as it did to her, or was it merely a diversion for him—something he could laugh about with the other skaters when he joined them in Florida?

After a half hour of roughhousing on the family room floor, they all gathered around the kitchen table.

"I'll pray," Becca offered as she clapped her hands.

"No, me!" Bobby volunteered as he smiled at Dan.

Dan grinned mischievously. "No! Let me!"

All eyes turned his direction.

"Hearing you three pray reminded me of a prayer my grandmother taught me when I was little. I'd nearly forgotten it. But I think I can say it." He looked directly at his hostess for permission. "May I?"

She nodded, bowed her head, and folded her hands.

Nervously, he began. "God is great and God is good. Let us thank Him for this food. By His hand. . ." He paused as if he'd forgotten the next words.

Becca peeked at Dan with one open eye and filled in, "We are fed!" then closed it again quickly.

"We are fed," he repeated with a muffled laugh. "Give us Lord, our daily bread." He raised his head proudly, as if he expected them to clap.

Something in Carlee's heart, a still small voice, seemed to say, *Don't give up. There's hope.*

The young couple sat gazing quietly into the fire after the children had been tucked into their beds. It seemed they no longer felt the need to talk to enjoy one another's company. It was enough to sit side by side, his arm about her shoulders and just be together.

"I've had a great evening. I love chili and the kids, but I've got to git."

"Chili and the kids? Sounds like a rock group when you say it that way." She grinned and snuggled her head onto his shoulder, savoring the moment. "Do you have to go?"

He stroked her hair, then stood. "We both have to get up early."

Carlee jumped up beside him, threw both arms about his waist, and squeezed tightly. He lowered his arms and thrust them about her shoulders. There they stood, motionless, embracing one another, neither understanding exactly why. They just wanted to do it. It felt right.

Dan cradled her chin with one hand while the other continued to hold her close, then lifted her face toward his. As if instructed by some unseen director, their faces moved slowly toward each other until their lips met, drawn by an invisible magnetism. But only for a moment. They separated quickly, as if they'd been taking something not theirs to take. Something forbidden.

"Oh, Dan." Carlee covered her face with her hands as she spoke. "We shouldn't be doing this. I'm too old to have a three-week fling. And I have children to consider. . . ."

He moved toward her, but she backed away.

"Maybe it'd be better if Father Bennett and I switched times until you leave. I can't bear to see you every day—to be so close to you. It's tearing my heart out."

"Carlee, we have so little time to be together. It's hard for me, too. I don't have any magical answers; I just know I want to be with you every moment I can. Please don't throw away what little time we have left; it's too precious!"

He took one more step toward her, and she nearly leaped into his arms. For an awkward moment they stood there, holding one another, their bodies pressed together in a warm embrace.

"Carlee," he whispered softly into her hair, "if you tell me to go, I'll leave Kansas City tomorrow and you'll never see me again. I don't want to hurt you."

"I–I know. . . ," she murmured weakly, all resistance gone.

He smiled that endearing smile that tore at her heart and caused her knees to go weak. "Last chance. What'll it be?"

"Oh, Dan—stay!"

His lips grazed her forehead, then lightly touched each eyelid, then the tip of her nose.

Her heart pounded wildly as his mouth sought hers and found it. How many times had she dreamed of this moment? Longed for it? Willed it to happen?

"Oh, Dan," she breathed in surrender. Never had a kiss been so sweet. It was more than she'd ever dreamed it would be, even if it had to last a lifetime after he was gone.

He held Carlee's hand as they walked slowly to the door. She bent slightly, and he kissed her on the top of her head as if she were Becca, then again drew her to him and kissed her tenderly with a kiss that brought out long-forgotten feelings of desire she'd thought had been extinguished forever.

She touched his lips with her fingertips and smiled with her eyes. "You will be skating tomorrow morning, won't you?"

"I'd rather go to church with you, if you'll let me tag along." His hands slowly stroked her spine.

Standing on tiptoes, she slipped one arm about his neck, and with an adoring smile, she kissed his cheek. "Good night, Dan. See you here at 10:15. And don't be late."

One final squeeze and he backed toward the door and closed it quietly behind him.

Carlee stared at the door. Dan was going to church with her and it was his own idea. Praise the Lord!

thirteen

Dan Castleberry caught an early morning glimpse of himself in the rearview mirror and smoothed his hair with his hand. Who would have thought he'd be attending church while in Kansas City? Twice, no less! And that he'd invite himself? He shook his head as he made a left-hand turn onto her street, then smiled, remembering the kisses he and Carlee had shared the night before. Deep in thought, he nearly missed Carlee's driveway. There she was in the open doorway, looking even more beautiful than she had the day before.

"Hi," she called out as she pulled the door shut behind her and tested the lock. "What a beautiful Lord's Day!"

Dan leaped out the door of his car, jumped the hedge, and met her at the foot of the steps. "Yeah, great, isn't it? By the way, you look terrific in red—you should wear it more often."

Her face flushed as she adjusted the shoulder strap of her bag. "Thank you. Somehow I felt like red this morning." She flipped the tip of his red paisley tie with her fingertips. "Looks like you did, too."

They laughed and talked and held hands all the way to the church. He in his red silk tie, she in her red wool suit. Becca and Bobby attacked Dan as the couple entered the lobby, and as the children expected, he swooped them both up in his strong arms and carried them into the sanctuary.

Carlee slid into the pew first, then Dan. He lowered Bobby down next to him. She tried to pull Becca from Dan's arms, but the little girl clung to his neck fiercely. "You promised I could sit next to Dan," she said in that loud, shrill baby voice of hers. People around them peeked over their hymnals and stared in amusement.

At the end of the service, church members shook hands with Dan and greeted him by name, as if he were a part of them. Jim caught his arm and pulled him to one side while Carlee visited with a group of women. "Hear you're going to the lake tomorrow. Good idea, son! You guys enjoy the day!" He gave Dan a hearty handshake and disappeared to find Ethel.

The Bennetts had been invited to a friend's house for the day, so Dan, Carlee, Bobby, and Becca went out for Mexican food. Then, after delivering them to their doorstep, Dan went on to his parents' house for the last Sunday he'd spend with them for a long time.

❧

Monday's weather promised to be as glorious as Sunday morning's had been. It was still dark when Dan and Carlee arrived at the Ice Palace, but the air had lost its nip and was perfectly still. The two walked arm in arm to the door as Dan related his day with his parents. Once inside the rink, he caught hold of her waist and spun her around. "Why don't we do it differently today? You know—break the routine."

She had no idea what he meant and raised her eyebrows questioningly.

"I'll make the coffee; you get the skates!" He placed his big hands on her shoulders. She backed off and grinned. "Sure. I'm game if you are." Then, gesturing toward the snack bar and the waiting coffeepot, she added, "Have at it."

The coffee was awful, but she drank it anyway. He took one sip, gagged, turned and spat it on the ice.

"That's terrible!" he shouted as he grabbed the cup from her hand. "Don't drink that stuff; you might get sick and miss our picnic." His hands waved in the air in frustration. "How hard can it be to make coffee? What did I do wrong?"

Carlee pressed her lips together, determined not to make fun of his efforts. "Maybe it was the water. Hmm. Looks like you did everything right except for one thing." She lifted the plastic basket from the coffeemaker.

He looked puzzled. "What?"

In her hand she held a ruffled, circular piece of white paper. "You forgot to put the filter in."

The practice session went well as the two waltzed gracefully around the ice. Dan was pleased with his progress.

Ethel greeted them at the door when they went by to pick up the children. "If you'd been a minute longer I would have had to tie them up," she said as she pointed to her grandchildren doing somersaults in the hallway at Dan's feet. "They were up at six and have been bouncing off the walls ever since. You'd think they'd never been on a picnic."

Dan pounced on the two wiggle worms, clutching one in each arm and holding them tight. They squealed with delight.

"Ready to head to the lake when you are," Carlee called out cheerfully as she headed for the front door, leaving Dan with two rambunctious wigglers in his arms.

"Hey, wait! Don't leave me with these squirmers," he pled as he hurried through the hall, carrying his precious cargo.

Dan was so good with the children, Carlee found it difficult to believe he hadn't been around kids all his life. According to him, he'd never even held a child before, yet he did it so naturally. And the kids loved him.

She scooted into the seat next to Dan, fastened her seat belt, and eyed the man behind the steering wheel; she was already hopelessly in love with him. As she touched her lips, she remembered the kisses they'd shared the night before—the kisses she'd longed for since that first day he'd invaded her life. If only Dan's career didn't keep him on the road fifty weeks a year. If only he'd allow God to take charge of his life. If, if, if. Too many ifs. They had the here and now, but there was no future for them. She knew it, and she was sure Dan must feel it too.

"What?" Dan asked when he caught her studying him.

She lifted one finger to her lips. "Shh! They're asleep. Enjoy the silence while you can." She stretched her arms and gave way to an exaggerated yawn.

"Early morning skating getting you down?"

She wiggled her shoulders as she rotated her head in small circles. "Not the early part. I hate to admit it, but my muscles are sore. You're making me use muscles I haven't used for a long time."

He moved his hand to her neck and began to massage it with his strong but gentle fingers. "Too rough?"

"Ohh. That feels so good. Be careful or I'll start purring. Mmm." She dropped her chin to her chest and enjoyed the firm kneading of her sore neck and shoulders. "Don't wear your hands out; you may have to continue this later," she cautioned as she cradled her hand over his and pulled it into her lap. His fingers entwined hers and stayed there. For several moments neither spoke nor looked at the other.

It was Carlee who finally broke the silence. "Dan," she said slowly and deliberately, as though something were weighing heavily on her mind. "I know this is probably all fun and games to you. . ."

He gave her hand an affectionate squeeze.

"What I'm trying to say, Dan, is that the children and I have loved having you here in Kansas City, spending time in our home. I know you'll probably forget all about us once you get back to the show—"

"And?" He shot a questioning glance her way, then turned his attention back to the road.

"Ohhh," she moaned, disgusted with her inability to express her feelings. "I don't know what I mean. I've been confused since the first day I met you." She tried to pull her hand away, but he wouldn't let her, tightening his grip.

"Look, Carlee, I'll be honest with you. I selected Kansas

City for one reason—to spend time with my folks. Fortunately, the Ice Palace afforded me the opportunity to do that and practice my skating at the same time. I never expected to meet you. Or your family. You came as a total surprise—a nice one!" He tapped the button on the cruise control and leaned back. "I've felt quite intimidated by you."

"By me?" How could he be intimidated by her?

"Yes. By you. I've never met anyone as—well, the only way I can think to put it is—pure. Yes, that's it. The word 'saint' comes to mind when I think of Carlee Bennett."

She gasped. "Me? Pure? A saint? Hardly, Dan!"

He grinned nervously. "Don't interrupt me, please."

"But—"

"Like I was saying, I felt intimidated. I've never dated a girl like you. Oh, I don't mean married with children. I mean someone with your morals and high standards. I have to confess, I wish I'd known years ago what I know now."

"But, Dan. Don't you understand? It isn't morals and high standards. It's God! I don't have a list of dos and don'ts. I didn't stay a virgin because I had set a high standard for myself, or wanted to be Miss Goody-Two-Shoes, whatever that means. I stayed a virgin because I knew God wanted me to, and I knew He'd help me resist temptation. Don't get the idea that Robert and I were never tempted, because we were. Constantly!"

Her voice dropped suddenly. What was she saying? She'd never told anyone about the temptations they'd faced when she and Robert were dating, not even her best friend. Yet, here she was, spilling her guts to a man she'd probably never hear from once he left Kansas City.

Dan let go of her hand, put his arm about her shoulders, and drew her close to his side.

She wanted to be near him, to feel his body next to hers. If only she could make him understand. "Dan, I don't know why I told you about Robert and me. I'm sorry. I should never have brought it up."

He pressed his lips to the top of her head, then concentrated on the road again. "Carlee, let me say something I've been wanting to get off my chest. I decided when I was a young teen that I was going to have a career as a professional skater. You know about my goals—I spent all my free time at the local rink, skating and honing my craft. I decided early on that girls could only get in my way.

"When I was in the ninth grade, one of the guys in my class got a girl pregnant. They ended up getting married four months later when they were fifteen. That scared me so bad I avoided girls like chicken pox. But the first year I was with the show, when I was nineteen, I dated the daughter of the show's owner. We got pretty serious; I guess mainly because I was in awe of her father. Well, one thing led to another and you can guess what happened. She told me she was pregnant. That really shook me up! I could see my whole career going down the tubes. I hated myself for my weakness and what I'd done to her. Then she called me and said she'd lied—she wasn't pregnant after all. Well, let me tell you, I ended things real fast! We broke up and I know you probably won't believe this, but she was the first and last girl I. . ."

She felt a great sense of relief wash through her; for some reason she'd always assumed he was a man of the world with many conquests, but there had been only one.

Dan sighed, gave her shoulders a quick rub, and continued. "I've never been intimate with a girl since. Honest! I hope you'll believe me; it's important that you do."

She lifted her face to his and looked into the eyes of the man she'd come to know so well in such a short time. "I do believe you, Dan," she said earnestly as tears welled up in her eyes and trickled down her cheeks. "And I'm glad you told me." She straightened and kissed his cheek tenderly.

They rode along in silence. She could forgive Dan for his improper behavior with his teenage girlfriend. And God would forgive him, too. But first Dan had to realize he was a sinner and needed God's forgiveness. But was he ready to do that?

fourteen

Becca woke up and began chattering about the cows and horses grazing in the fields. Dan and Carlee sat quietly in the front seat, holding hands just out of sight of the children.

"Okay, troops," Dan said, "the lake is around the next curve in the road. We're almost there."

Suddenly there it was—a huge, beautiful lake, sparkling in the afternoon sun like a million diamonds. He turned off the highway onto a gravel road, then pulled up next to a concrete picnic table and stopped. Without a word, he opened the trunk and removed a stack of raggedy old quilts and a picnic basket. Two giggling children dropped onto the nearest quilt when he spread it out on the ground. Dan snapped a second quilt high into the air and lowered it like an open parachute. Carlee leaned against the car and watched, spellbound. "You think of everything. Wherever did you get such wonderful old quilts?"

He lowered himself onto a quilt and motioned for her to join him. "Borrowed them from Mrs. Sweeney," he answered with a chuckle as he began pulling food from the picnic basket.

After a satisfying lunch, the young couple settled onto one of the quilts while the children explored the shoreline and tossed rocks into the water.

Dan pulled the remaining quilt around the two of them, and there they sat in the center of the fraying red-and-blue Ohio Star quilt, covered snugly, with Carlee enfolded in Dan's arms. Two boats lazily crossed the big lake, dragging sagging fishing lines behind them, as the young couple watched. Three white egrets stood in the water, close to the shore, like statues. The two watched as the pristine birds moved forward cautiously, first on one foot, then the other, effortlessly, gracefully, barely breaking the water's surface.

"Look," Dan whispered as he hugged her close. "There. . . by the tree. Two little brown rabbits." Dan and Carlee sat so still, the rabbits wandered unbelievably close before they spotted the two humans and bounced away.

Carlee nestled her head under his chin. "Oh, Dan. This is the stuff real life is made of. God created all of this for our pleasure." Overhead, hawks circled, lazily gliding heavenward on unseen winds, while two children chased one another along the ragged shoreline.

"Carlee, what we were talking about earlier—I'd like to talk about it some more."

She nodded her head.

"Knowing you has caused some real problems in my life. I've. . ." He stopped.

She could feel her heart thundering in her chest and was sure he could feel it, too.

"I've—fallen in love with you."

Her heart did a flip-flop this time. That was the last thing she expected to hear him say. She felt breathless, unable to speak. All she could do was lift her head to face him in awe.

He pulled several pieces of dried grass from her hair. "I have, Carlee—deeply in love. I love you; I love the kids. I've finally admitted it to myself, but I don't know what to do about it. I can't give up my skating career; it means too much to me. I've worked too hard to achieve what I've got."

A heron swooped and soared overhead, but neither noticed. Carlee wanted to respond, to say something, anything, but the words wouldn't come. All she could do was pray.

"And I can't ask you to follow me from city to city; that would be impossible with the children. I would never do that to them, or to you. Even if you home-schooled on the road, it would be too hard for them to pick up and move every few days, or weeks at most."

Her heart burst with love, yet ached with grief. What could she say?

"And I realize that isn't our only problem. Your God is important to you; your life is based on your being a Christian. I'm not even sure what that is."

She flung her arms about his neck and buried her head in his chest. She knew if she tried to speak, to tell him of her feelings and misgivings, she'd cry. She loved him so much. More than she'd realized. And like him, she'd been fighting her feelings and trying to deny them. This was the most open he'd been about the lack of a relationship with God.

He lifted her face to his and searched misty eyes. "Carlee! Say something. I need to know what you're feeling."

"Oh, Dan! I love you, too. My heart is so full of love for you, I think it will burst. Hearing your words, knowing that you love me, too, makes me so happy!" She gulped and wiped at her eyes with the back of her hand. "I've been thinking about the same things you have. Only I thought it was all a selfish dream; I had no idea you could love me. I fantasized about your love but never dared hope my dreams could come true."

He pulled her trembling body close to his own and smothered her eager, receptive mouth with sweet, tender kisses. She wound her arms around his neck and responded eagerly, returning each glorious kiss, her love for him taking command of the moment. If only this precious afternoon could last forever. A deep sigh made its way to the surface and erupted as fantasy was displaced by reality. "Oh, Dan! What are we going to do? Is there any hope for us?"

He pulled away from her and scanned her face as he pushed strands of hair, damp from her tears, off her lovely face. His own troubled countenance said it all—he had no answers. Their lives seemed to run on parallel tracks, side by side, but never coming together. "I don't know, Carlee. I just don't know," he confessed. "I only know I love you and want to spend my life with you. But how?"

They sat, locked in one another's arms, savoring every moment of their time together—time that was rushing past them rapidly. Five more days and it would be over.

"Why are you crying, Mama?" Becca asked as she climbed onto the quilt. "Did you hurt yourself?"

Dan wiped Carlee's tears away with his fingertips. "Mama's okay, Becca," he said as he pulled the little girl onto his lap. "Don't worry, honey. Dan's gonna take care of your mother." He gave Carlee's shoulders a squeeze. "He just doesn't know how."

He folded the quilts and loaded them and the picnic basket into the trunk while Carlee helped the children into the car and fastened their seat belts. He clung to Carlee's hand as they drove back to Kansas City, as if he were afraid he'd lose her forever if he loosened his grip.

She smiled and leaned close to him. "I love you, Dan," she whispered softly in his ear as he drove.

"I love you, Carlee," he mouthed silently as he kept his eyes on the road.

The children chattered all the way home, but Carlee and Dan scarcely heard a word the children said as they continued to sit silently in the front seat, holding hands, conscious of the few fleeting days they had left.

☙

Dan Castleberry stood quietly by Becca's bed, staring at the little girl's sleeping face—so sweet and peaceful, so innocent—and wondered what it would be like to hear her call him "Daddy." He'd never thought of himself as daddy material. But now, standing by Becca, he longed to hear those words from her tiny pink lips. He turned to see Carlee leaning against the doorway. "You have a beautiful daughter, Mrs. Bennett," he whispered as he slipped his arm about her waist and led her from the room.

As they passed Bobby's room, Dan leaned inside for a final peek at the boy. It was time for him to leave, but he couldn't separate himself from this family and the pleasure he'd experienced just being with them. Despite the joy they'd shared, he felt a sense of despair, a finality, hanging like a black cloud over them.

&

Carlee found it next to impossible to sleep. Dan's words kept filtering through her mind. *I love you, Carlee. I love you, Carlee.* They echoed over and over again, words she'd longed for but never expected to hear. When she would drift off to sleep she would dream the words, hearing Dan's voice somewhere in the distance. *I love you, Carlee.* But each time she ran toward him, he would retreat, then begin calling to her once again. She'd run, but fall to the ground breathless, never quite able to reach him.

&

Dan Castleberry twisted and turned in his bed, pulling the covers about his shoulders one minute and casting them off the next. Sleep eluded him as thoughts of Carlee filled his weary mind. His life had been so simple, so structured before he'd come to Kansas City. Now confusion reigned. He'd been secure in what he wanted and expected out of life. A wife and ready-made family had never been part of that picture. Yet now, that was exactly what he wanted. The only trouble was, he wanted his skating career, too.

&

The two arrived at the rink at the same time Tuesday morning. They stood in the parking lot in the cool early morning air and embraced. Dan lifted Carlee's face to his and kissed her cheeks, her eyelids, her neck, then her lips—the perfect way for lovers to start the day.

Their skating was even more in sync than it had been the day before, and Carlee was glad she was able to please Dan with her skating ability. She held up her head proudly as they twirled and dipped across the ice to the music, his arm encircling her waist. When the hour was up, Dan slipped the protective rockers onto their skates, took her hand, and led her silently across the lobby to a chair. Unspoken words passed between them as they gazed into one another's eyes. Dan stooped and lifted Carlee's foot onto his knee and began unlacing the boot of her skate.

"You don't have to do that," she said with a slight frown as she tried to withdraw it from his grasp.

He clung fast to the leather boot and lifted sad eyes to meet hers. "I want to, Carlee. I want to do everything I can for you—our time is so short." He lowered his eyes and continued to remove her skates, then slipped her tennies onto her stockinged feet.

She watched this man kneeling before her, her Prince Charming. He would always be that to her, even if she never saw him again once this week was over. She leaned toward him, placed her arms about his neck, and planted a kiss in his dark locks. "I know, Dan. I know."

Dan's parents had requested that he spend the rest of the day with them. He phoned her late that evening and, after they'd talked about the day's happenings, Dan repeated the words he'd spoken on the picnic trip. "I love you, Carlee."

She took a deep breath and leaned into the plumped pillows she'd propped against the headboard of her bed. "I love you, Dan. I never thought I'd say those words—after Robert. But I mean them with my whole heart. I love you."

With a long, slow sigh, he stretched out across his bed and gazed at the ceiling. "What are we going to do about it?"

❧

Dan drummed his fingers on the dashboard of his car

Wednesday morning. He'd hoped Carlee would arrive early too. He had to see her—had to spend every waking moment with her. How had he let himself get into this predicament? He'd fallen in love so fast he hadn't seen it coming—it just happened. He was hopelessly, totally in love.

❧

Carlee drove down Clark Street. She considered how the past two days had changed her life. Dan Castleberry had proclaimed his love for her, and for the first time she'd admitted, not only to Dan but to herself, that she was in love with him. Despite the dilemma their love caused, it was a joy to have their feelings out in the open. But could she compromise her convictions? Dan was one of the finest men she'd ever known, but he'd made it clear he wasn't interested in letting God rule his life. Even if they could find a way to be together, dare she marry a man who didn't love her Lord the way she did? Maybe in time he would accept God on God's terms, but could she count on it? Hadn't the Scriptures warned against that? True; Dan's career seemed an insurmountable obstacle, but so was his lack of relationship with God. How many women had married men expecting them to change and found that they didn't? Too many, for sure. What about the influence of such a man on her children? A man without the same convictions about rearing children in the church?

No, as much as she loved Dan, she could never compromise; her children were too important. God had seen fit to make her both mother and father to them. He had entrusted them to her. She would not fail God. But, why worry about it? With Dan's career in their way anyway, she'd never have to face that problem. She'd relish each minute she could spend with him now, and when Dan left Kansas City, things would come to an end and all she'd have left would be the wonderful memories. Precious memories of the times they'd spent together. She should probably end things now, before any more emotional damage was done. But she couldn't! She loved him too much. She had to be with him as long as she could. "Oh, God. . .make me strong!"

As she watched him skate she tried to envision the number he would skate in the new show. Perhaps he'd wear a long cape over his broad shoulders. It would spread out like wings as he moved like silent wind across the ice, thrilling appreciative audiences with his skillfully executed jumps and spins. Maybe there would be fog whirling about his feet, as there had been in Snow White.

She thought of Valerie Burns and was filled with envy. It would be Valerie who would be held in Dan's arms, who would feel his closeness. No doubt; there would be places in the program that called for the Beast to kiss Belle and Valerie would be smothered with his kisses, instead of her. She shivered at the thought.

"Cold?" he asked as he stepped off the ice.

She blushed guiltily. "No, just thinking."

He eyed her suspiciously, then pulled her to her feet and wrapped his arms about her. "About what? What would make you shiver like that?"

She clung tightly, basking in the protective strength that emanated from him, savoring the moment, a moment she'd cherish long after he was gone. "It's not important."

The young couple spent the day together. Mother Bennett had offered to watch the children till bedtime. Dan helped with the bookwork, then the morning session. They worked well together, like a well-oiled machine. The time went quickly.

Lunchtime found them at a nearby McDonald's, sharing French fries and sipping chocolate shakes like two infatuated teenagers. Dan watched as Carlee methodically dipped the tip of each fry in catsup before popping it into her mouth. Carlee smiled as Dan doused his fries with salt. Just being together made their meal as special as the most elaborate banquet. He wiped a dot of catsup from her chin with his napkin as she grinned at her hero.

After lunch they headed for the Plaza to select a gift for Mrs. Castleberry's birthday. Dan wanted to get something really special for his mom. It had been five years since he'd been home to celebrate the occasion with her.

"What should I get?" he asked as he pulled into the parking lot. "I end up wiring flowers every year, mostly because I'm on the road and it's the easiest thing to do. I don't want to do that same old thing, since I'm here in Kansas City. Any suggestions?"

Carlee looked thoughtful. "Does she like beautiful linens? You know, like tablecloths and napkins?"

A puzzled look revealed how little Dan knew about his mother.

"How about perfumes? No," she said, shaking her head, "that's too personal a choice when you don't know what a woman likes. Let's see. . ." She touched her fingers to her chin and stared off into space. "Jewelry? Dresser set? Handbag?"

He shoved his hands into his pockets. "Don't know. It's hard to choose something she'd like. She's pretty picky."

Carlee was glad he wanted this gift to be special; she felt she could tell a lot about a man by the way he treated his mother. Whatever his gift would be, it had to be just right. But what? Her face brightened.

"Dan! Do you have a good photo of yourself? Maybe skating and wearing one of your costumes?"

He studied her face. "Why?"

"Just answer. Do you?"

"Sure. Publicity shots. All skaters have those."

"A recent one? From here in Kansas City?"

He had no idea what she was leading up to. "Yes, in my briefcase. I have several four by five shots."

"Then I think I've got it!" she said, her eyes twinkling with excitement. "We'll take one to a photo-processing place and get it blown up to poster size and have it framed for her. She'd love it. Any mother would. What do you think?"

"Do you really think she'd like it? A picture of me?"

"Yes, Dan. I do."

He grinned, delighted with the idea. "Let's do it!"

They drove to his parents' house on Ward Parkway, just minutes from the Plaza. As usual, they were out. Carlee stood on the expansive porch of the grand, ivy-covered brick mansion as Dan fumbled for his key. "Dan, I've admired these lovely homes on Ward Parkway as long as I've lived in Kansas City. I never expected to know anyone who actually lived in one."

"They don't! Live, I mean. They exist here. You live in a *home*. They exist in a house."

He led her into the magnificent foyer with its marbled floors and gilded mirrors. She stared at her reflection, smoothing her hair and straightening the lapels on her jacket.

Dan moved up behind her, slipped his arm around her waist, and peered over her shoulder. "Mirror, mirror, on the wall. Who is the fairest of them all?"

The beginning of a smile turned up the corners of her mouth. "I bite. Who? Valerie Burns?"

"You, my love. Don't move a hair; you look beautiful just the way you are." He rubbed his chin against her neck.

"I know what you're thinking, Carlee. But you're wrong. I hated this place; still do. It was like living in a museum. No place to raise a boy. Bobby doesn't know how lucky he is. I'd have much preferred his life to mine. His mother puts her children first. I got leftovers from my mother's life. She just couldn't fit me in on her calendar." Dan pulled the photo from the briefcase and reluctantly handed it to Carlee. "Are you sure this is a good idea? What if she thinks it's a joke?"

She grabbed the picture from his hand and gazed at the handsome image staring back at her. "It's perfect."

They located the photo-processing center and left the photo for enlarging and framing.

"One jumbo fresh cherry limeade," Dan barked into the microphone when they stopped at a drive-in restaurant on the way back to Carlee's house. "With two straws, please."

They held the big container between the two of them and sipped as fifties music boomed from speakers hanging under the metal canopy. When the last drop was gone, Dan removed the plastic lid, retrieved the long-stemmed maraschino cherry, and offered it to Carlee. She grinned, then bit it from the stem.

He scrunched down in the seat and rested his head on the seat back. "It's Wednesday, Carlee."

She scooted close to him, her head against his shoulder. "I know," she said softly, her voice filled with emotion.

The jukebox was playing a love song. "Please release me, let me go," the crooner sang. Dan hummed along as they listened to the words. "You're going to have to, you know," he murmured as his fingers tightened around hers. "I'm your captive."

She pressed against him. "It's the other way around. You're going to have to release me. You're the strong one. You'll have to walk away from me, Dan. I may not have the strength to let you go."

For minutes they sat silently, oblivious to the cars parked on either side of them. Time was rapidly ticking away.

❧

Dan had driven Carlee to the grocery store to pick up bread and lettuce for Bobby's school lunch box. He watched now as she moved from the pantry to the refrigerator, putting things away.

"Water?" she asked as she took glasses from the cupboard.

He nodded, then watched as she filled them with ice and

wondered what it would be like to share a home with her, to wake up to her each morning and help her with the dishes, buy groceries, do married-folk stuff. She was so. . .*comfortable*. Yes, that was the word for it. No pretenses. He was that way, too—when he was around her. So much of his life was lived on stage, performing in a role before an audience. People didn't know the real man or care who he was; they just wanted to be entertained. But Carlee was different. He knew she respected his talent as a skater, but he didn't have to be on stage with her. He could be Dan Castleberry, the man. And when he was with her, he felt like a man. She brought out his best, and he liked that.

"Dan? Ho, Dan! Where are you?" Her hand passed in front of his eyes, bringing him back to reality.

He grabbed her wrist, pulled it to his face, and kissed her palm affectionately. "I was thinking about you. About us."

For supper, they phoned for pizza. Afterward, Dan cleared away the mess and took it to the kitchen. Carlee was kneeling before the blazing fireplace, deep in thought, when he returned. He knelt behind her and used his strong fingers to manipulate her shoulders, kneading the muscles gently with his thumbs. "Tight," he murmured into her ear. "Relax."

"Umm. Wonderful," she purred. "Don't ever stop."

His hands moved smoothly from her shoulders to her back. "I don't want to stop. I love touching you."

"Oh, Dan. Why did we ever let things go this far? We both knew we were doomed from the beginning."

The room filled with silence, except for the crackling of the fire and the pounding of two hearts. Dan cradled Carlee in his arms and held her there as they stared into the flames and envisioned their dreams going up in smoke. Their love was at a standstill. It had nowhere to go. In three days, it would be nothing but a memory.

fifteen

Dan picked up Carlee at five A.M. Thursday. After their skating session, he swept the snack bar floor, did a few repairs around the rink that Jim hadn't had time to do, and sharpened four pair of skates for customers as they waited. It was nearly noon before he and Carlee's paths crossed again.

"Father Bennett'll be surprised when he sees all the things you've done around here," she said proudly as she locked the door behind them. "It's a pretty big job for one man, running a rink like this. Are you sure you can't stick around? I'll bet he'd hire you as his right-hand man."

"Don't tempt me," he warned as he opened the car door and motioned her in. "I'm so crazy about you, if he asked me right now, I'd probably take him up on it."

With a melancholy look, she slid to the center of the front seat. "Oh, Dan, don't talk like that; your career is important to you. As much as I love you and want to be with you, I'm sure you'd always resent giving it all up."

They waited at the Castleberry house for nearly two hours before his mother arrived home. They'd propped up the poster-sized photo of Dan on the grand piano, and Carlee was admiring it when they heard the front door open and Dan's mother step inside.

"Happy Birthday, Mother!" Dan sang out cheerfully.

She reared back. "Daniel. You know I hate birthdays."

He pushed Carlee forward. "Mother, this is Carlee Bennett. She and her in-laws own the rink where I've been practicing my new routines. We've become—friends."

Mrs. Castleberry was so engrossed in removing her gloves,

she paid little attention to the introduction.

"It's nice to meet you, Mrs. Castleberry. Dan was so pleased he'd be here in Kansas City for your birthday."

The elder woman smoothed her French twist as she lowered herself into a white brocade chair. "Oh, yes. When is it you are leaving, Daniel? I've forgotten."

Carlee nudged his elbow and whispered, "The photo, Dan."

Dan lifted the photo from the piano and held it before his mother, beaming at his gift. "For you, Mother. Happy Birthday. I hope you like it."

The older woman sat staring at the handsome likeness of her son. "Daniel, whatever will I do with that huge thing?"

He looked devastated. Her words cut deeply into Dan's heart. He had so hoped to make her birthday special. He stood before her, disappointment etched on his face. "I'm sorry, Mother. Next time I'll wire flowers. If you don't like them, I won't know it, because I won't be here."

"Now, Daniel, you needn't be smart with me. You don't want to embarrass yourself in front of your little friend."

He tossed the frame onto the floor, grasped Carlee by the hand, and pulled her toward the front door. "Good-bye, Mother. Happy Birthday," he said coolly as he slammed the door behind him and they left the Castleberry mansion. Once outside, Dan pulled Carlee into his arms and held her so tightly she had to struggle for breath.

"Oh, Dan. It was all my fault. I'm the one who encouraged you to give her that picture. I can't bear to see you hurt like this. I am so sorry!" She wrapped her arms around him and stroked his cheek with her fingers.

"No, Carlee. I'm the one who's sorry. Sorry you had to be a part of that fiasco. I know my mother well enough to have expected her to behave like that. She's been that way all my life. A selfish, vain woman."

Carlee stood on tiptoe and kissed him on the tip of his

nose. "She did one thing right. She gave birth to you."

He grinned, took a deep breath, and exhaled slowly. "Enough of that. Let's go celebrate her birthday our way. Without her!"

The two wrapped their arms about one another and walked toward the car. Time was too short to let Mrs. Castleberry's words ruin it for them. Her loss was Carlee's gain.

"Hey," Dan said suddenly as they turned into the Bennett driveway. "It's Thursday. Hot dog night! Do I hear an invitation for me to stay for supper?"

She grinned. "I might be persuaded to invite you."

ta

Bobby, Becca, and Dan wrestled on the floor while Carlee assembled the food items in the kitchen. The sound of laughter should have made her happy, but it didn't. She couldn't get the episode with Dan's mother off her mind. She'd never forget the hurt look on his face, the rejection in his eyes. What a miserable childhood he must have had. No wonder he joined the ice show at such an early age; his home life must have been nearly nonexistent.

When the hot dogs were roasted and ready to eat, Dan suggested they all sing Happy Birthday to his mother. Becca and Bobby loved singing the birthday song and were happy for any occasion to sing it. But they couldn't quite understand how you could sing a song to someone who wasn't there!

After the children were in bed, Dan slipped out the door while Carlee was busy clearing up the dishes.

"Got something for you," he said with an ornery grin as she finished in the kitchen. He put his arm around her waist and tugged her into the family room.

"It's not my birthday," she said, then wished she hadn't mentioned the "birthday" word.

He reached behind the sofa and pulled out a poster-sized photo, the same photo he'd given his mother.

"Here. For you," he said shyly. "I hope you like it better than my mother did. I had them make a second one."

Carlee's hand went over her mouth and she blinked back tears of joy. "Oh, Dan. I love it!" The smiling face of the man who had skated into her life gazed back at her. "You don't know what this means to me. How can I ever thank you?" She lovingly took the big picture from his hands and stood it on the fireplace mantel. "It's going to stay right here where the children and I can see it every day."

"You—uh—don't think it's too big? Would you rather have a smaller one—to go on your desk?"

"No, silly! And if your mother doesn't want hers, I'll be glad to take it off her hands and hang it on my bedroom wall—so I can keep my eye on you."

He hugged her to him and rubbed his cheek against her hair. Her home had become a haven for him since he'd arrived in Kansas City, a place filled with love and warmth and security. Instead of love for his mother, he felt pity. She and his father and all their fine friends worked hard at finding happiness in things. But Carlee and the Bennetts had found the true secret to happiness. And best of all, they were willing to share it with him.

The flickering flames in the fireplace seemed to draw the young lovers to it as it crackled and popped its invitation to come and bask in its warmth. Dan pulled plump sofa pillows onto the floor and leaned into them. Carlee dropped beside him and curved into his beckoning arms. Neither spoke. Words were no longer necessary. There was an unspoken language of love between them and they understood one another completely.

It was Carlee who broke the silence. "If you want, we can spend the last two days together. Mother Bennett offered to keep the children and Father Bennett said he'd take care of the rink."

Dan twisted a lock of her hair between his fingers and studied it intently. "Have you talked to them? About us?"

"Not really. But they know. I'm sure. They've always encouraged me to date. They want what's best for me."

"Oh, Carlee, Carlee. What have I done to you? I had no right to come into your life like this—with empty hands. I have nothing to offer you. Nothing but heartache."

Her fingertips pressed to his lips. "Hush! We did it together. I fell in love with you that very first morning you came to the rink. Neither of us was looking for the other. It just happened. It's no one's fault."

He sought her lips with his and kissed them tenderly as his hands caressed her back. Her lips tasted like fine honey from the comb.

His mind was awash in confusion. He had no future to offer her. None at all, with his lifestyle and career. Yet he wanted her more than anything he'd ever wanted. Wanted to marry her and be a father to her children. How could the most important things in his life be at such opposite ends of the spectrum? Maybe once he was away from all of this, he could forget her, put this all behind him. But in his heart he knew that would never happen.

"What if I give up skating?" he asked suddenly.

She look startled. "Give up skating? Give up your career? You'd never be happy, Dan. We both know that."

He traced her lips with his finger. "Then come with me, Carlee. We'll make it work, somehow. I love you!"

She shut her eyes tightly. "But the children. Oh, Dan—it would never work."

He watched as a lone tear escaped and ran down her cheek. "Is that the only reason, Carlee? Or is it also that I'm not a churchgoer? Are you afraid I might be a bad influence on your children?"

She appeared to be stung by his words. After a pause, she

answered, "Not your influence, my love; you're a wonderful, honorable man. But faith is an issue with me. You've been very courteous when we've had prayer in our home. You've even attended church with me. But you've never made any claim to be a Christian. We've always been honest with one another and I'll be honest with you now—I could never marry a man who did not love my Lord, even if all our other problems suddenly vanished."

He lowered his head thoughtfully. "Wow, you don't pull any punches!" He knew he'd never said no to God, but he hadn't said yes, either. Maybe he didn't fully understand what God and Carlee expected of him. "Carlee. . . ," he said, needing to change the subject, "I've been thinking. You know what I'd really like to do my last two days?" He sat back, erect, and turned her toward him. "You've told me you like to put up your Christmas decorations in early December. I'd like to help you. Maybe the four of us could go shop for a tree, string popcorn—whatever you usually do. Could we?"

Her eyes brightened. "What a great idea. Oh, yes!"

❧

She was waiting in the doorway with Ethel by her side when Dan drove in at five the next morning. She ran to the car, scooted close to Dan, and slipped her hand into his. "I've been thinking. . .about us. We can be miserable about you leaving or we can enjoy each moment we have together. I say, let's enjoy our time! What do you think?"

He was surprised and pleased; he'd been thinking the same thing during the wee hours of the morning when sleep had eluded him. "Sounds good to me."

"Okay," she began, her eyes filled with anticipation, "as soon as your practice is over, will you take me to breakfast at one of those all-you-can-eat places? I have this yearning for sausage, biscuits, gravy, pancakes, fruit—"

"Whoa!" he shouted. "What happened to moderation?

You're talking Fat City!"

She lifted her chin and drew in a deep breath. "Today I want to throw caution to the wind—and pig out!"

"Once we've gorged ourselves, then what?" He'd expected their remaining days to be difficult; apparently he'd been wrong.

Carlee's eyes sparkled. "Then we go find a tree! We can do it the easy way and go to a tree lot, or—"

"Or what?"

"We can drive out to a tree farm and cut our own!"

A frown furrowed his forehead as he considered the choices. "I say, let's cut our own! Now that that part's settled, what's our next project?" He angled his head toward hers and raised his brows.

"Mounting the tree in the stand and stringing the lights. You do know how to string lights, don't you?" She grinned.

"Want the truth?"

"Only the truth," she said as she jabbed his arm.

"I haven't the faintest idea how to do either. My parents hired someone to come in and decorate the house, including the tree. Is it hard?"

A serene smile blossomed on her face. "No, just takes time and effort. You'll do fine. I'll show you how."

That morning, he skated a flawless solo for an appreciative audience of one. When the music ended, he skated over to the front row, where she was waiting for him.

"Oh, Dan," Carlee said with a look of admiration as she reached both hands toward his. "That was beautiful!"

He cupped his hands over hers, lifted them to his lips, and kissed them passionately. "Sweetheart, your praise means more to me than that of any audience."

He'd called her "sweetheart" for the first time, and he'd said it so easily. She loved hearing it.

"Now," he instructed as he pulled her to him and onto the

ice. "It's your turn." They stood in the center of the ice, their arms entwined, as they waited for their pair number to begin.

"This is the last time we'll skate this number together, Carlee. At least for now." He pressed his chin against her forehead. She could feel the beating of his heart. "I love you, Carlee Bennett. Never forget it!"

The music started and they began to move as one, taking long, smooth strides across the gleaming ice, twisting and turning to the stains of a waltz. Never had Carlee skated as she did with Dan. There was something about being cradled in his arms that brought out the best of her skating ability. It was as though her feet never touched the ice but floated along beside him, moving as he moved, whirling as he whirled. They were poetry in motion. Their final skating session was the best one of all.

※

"The Christmas tree!" Becca squealed as she ran across the room and leaped into Dan's arms.

Bobby tossed his books onto the coffee table and stared at the perfectly shaped Scotch pine standing in the corner of the family room.

"I cut it and your mom helped me string the lights," Dan bragged, his face aglow with pride. "Now I'm going to plug in the lights. Everybody ready?"

"Ready!" Becca shouted as she clapped her little hands.

Carlee gathered her children on the sofa and the three watched expectantly as Dan ceremoniously pushed the plug into the socket. A mass of brilliant colors burst forth.

"Ohhhhh!" they said in unison.

"Dan, it's beautiful!" Carlee praised as she shot him an adoring glance.

Dan carried boxes of decorations from the attic, and the happy foursome spent the rest of the afternoon stringing popcorn and cranberries and placing ornaments on the tree.

They hung angels made from white paper plates and snowflakes cut from construction paper. They placed reindeer made from twigs on the entertainment center. Dan and Carlee cut branches from the evergreens in her backyard and draped them in an arch over the fireplace, then added a string of red lights and big red satin bows. The final touch was lining Carlee's lovely holiday dolls across the mantel. Becca shrieked with joy and clapped her hands each time a doll was put in its place. "See, Dan? I told you Mama got more Barbies than me. Aren't they pretty?"

He had to admit it—they *were* pretty. And the mantel was the perfect place to display them. The room looked magnificent, better than any Dan could remember as a child. A warmth filled him as he watched the children add the very last items to the tree—more of their homemade ornaments.

Carlee poked him gently in the ribs. "Aren't you wondering what's going to go on the coffee table? There's one more box on the shelf in the garage. Would you mind getting it?" And she added, "Be careful, it's fragile."

Dan retrieved the big box and carefully placed it on the floor by the coffee table. "What's in here?"

"You'll see." Cautiously she lifted the lid and began removing tissue-wrapped treasures from the box.

"It's a 'tivity, Dan," Becca declared with authority. "But don't touch—it will break if you do. No hands on it. Just look!"

Dan watched as Carlee carefully pulled the wrappings from Mary and Joseph and the baby Jesus, along with the wise men, shepherds, an angel, sheep, donkeys, and a cow. Last, she lifted the crude wooden manger from the box and placed it in the center of the polished tabletop. Her care with each figure amazed him and spoke worlds to him about her love for her Lord. His birth was the center of her Christmas. The tree and all the decorations took second place.

"I like your 'tivity, Becca," he said with misty eyes.

"Mama said He was borned and died for us," Becca said, her little chin resting on the table as she examined the baby Jesus figure.

"You gotta ask Him to come into your heart. Did you know that, Dan?" Bobby asked with childlike frankness as he dropped onto the floor by his little sister.

Dan flashed a glance at Carlee. "I'm beginning to understand that, Bobby," he said in an almost-whisper.

He tucked the children into bed after he'd told them one of his famous fairy tales, then joined Carlee in front of the fire. She'd turned off all the lights in the room except the Christmas lights. Dan reclined on the floor and gazed at the radiant tree. "I think that's the prettiest tree I've ever seen."

Carlee stretched out beside him. "When all the trees at your parents' house were decorated by professionals?"

He slipped an arm over her shoulders. "Those trees didn't compare with this one. And I sure wasn't allowed to hang paper-plate angels and construction-paper snowflakes on it!"

"The children and I loved having you here with us, helping us decorate the house. Thank you, Dan. You've made this day one I'll cherish forever." Her voice carried the same element of sadness as his.

It was well after midnight when Dan rose to go back to his parents' house. "I don't want to go, Carlee. This place is magical."

"I know," she whispered softly as she tucked her hand into his arm. "When you're here, it's magical for me, too." She could feel her heart thundering; she was so full of love for this man, she felt her heart would explode. She tried to remember how she'd felt about Robert. Had this same love filled her heart? It was so long ago, it was hard to remember. Maybe it was because she and Dan couldn't be together, like forbidden fruit, that made love so sweet now. Whatever it was, it was ripping her to shreds inside. The thought of his leaving twisted in her like the jab of a knife. How could love hurt so much?

They stood in the doorway as Dan prepared to leave, holding one another, kissing, hugging as though there were no tomorrow. But there would be a tomorrow. And it would be their final day together.

sixteen

Dan Castleberry had already told his parents good-bye and was packed and ready to go to the airport by the time he arrived at Carlee's house at seven A.M. for breakfast. Thanks to Jim, Carlee's family would be able to spend all day with Dan. Carlee had risen early and breakfast was well under way when he arrived.

"Oh, yummm," he moaned as he caught the aroma of bacon frying on the big electric griddle. The smell filled the house and made his taste buds jump to attention.

Bobby and Becca ran, giggling and happy, to Dan and wrapped themselves around his muscular legs. He gathered the two wiry children into his arms and carried them to the cozy kitchen where their mother was standing at the counter, using two forks to turn the sizzling strips on the griddle.

"Hi. Sleep well?" she asked, her heart thumping wildly.

He took one of the forks from her hand and flipped over two slices, then scooted them alongside the others. "Nope. Couldn't keep from thinking about you, honey," he whispered into her ear as he sidled up next to her and kissed her cheek.

"It was the same for me." She rested her head on his shoulder with a sigh of contentment.

Becca broke the spell. "Orange juice, please."

Dan moved to the refrigerator and poured a glass of juice for Becca, then filled the other glasses on the table. Bobby took a sip, put his elbows on the tablecloth, and propped up his head with his hands, his lower lip drooping sadly. "Do you have to go, Dan? Can't you stay here with us?"

Dan pulled a chair up next to the boy's and put his hand on the lad's shoulder. "Wish I could, Bobby, but I've got to get back to my job with the ice show. I'd take you and Becca and your mom with me, but how would you go to school? I move from city to city every week or so. We've tried, but your mom and I can't think of any way it would work out."

Carlee lowered her eyes and absentmindedly moved the bacon around on the grill. "Bobby, it's very important for Dan to skate in the show; that's how he makes his living. He's a big star. You wouldn't want him to give that up, would you?"

Without hesitation, Bobby replied, "If he could stay with us, I would!"

The two tried to explain to Bobby what "career" meant and why it was important to Dan, but all he knew was that Dan would be leaving and he didn't like it one bit. Neither did Becca.

They shared the big breakfast Carlee had prepared, laughing and talking about everything except Dan's leaving. Carlee couldn't face another discussion on that subject. His leaving was inevitable, and that was that.

The children watched a Saturday-morning cartoon while Dan helped Carlee clean the kitchen. "Carlee, don't move! Stay right where you are. I want to take a mental picture of you here in your kitchen, the place I've spent some of the best hours of my life."

She gnawed at her lower lip and feigned a smile. "Oh, Dan. I'll think of you each time I come into this room, or the family room, and remember the great times we've had with you. You've been such an important part of our lives."

"Have been?" He crossed the highly polished kitchen floor, threw his arms around her, and held her close, rubbing her smooth cheek with his freshly shaven face. "Please don't say that; it sounds so—final!"

The children were still watching cartoons when the two

moved into the family room. Dan sat in the corner of the couch and placed his feet onto the ottoman. Carlee plumped the pillows, sat down beside him, and snuggled in as close as she could. They silently enjoyed each other's nearness as they watched the lights blinking on the Christmas tree, casting reflections on the shiny ornaments and tinsel.

Ethel and Jim came over to say their good-byes. Jim took Dan aside and they talked quietly in hushed tones. When they'd gone, Carlee questioned Dan. "What were you and Father Bennett so secretive about?"

Dan appeared thoughtful but would only say, "Man talk."

For lunch Carlee prepared one of Dan's favorites—a chicken enchilada casserole with chips and a green salad—then served homemade deep-dish cherry pie for dessert. He reclined in the big chair, with Bobby and Becca cuddled on his lap, while Carlee cleaned the kitchen. He'd offered to help, but she suggested he spend the time with the children before she sent them over to the Bennetts for the rest of the day. His remaining time would be hers alone. When the children had gone, she stood before him and held out her arms. "Hold me, Dan. Please."

He rushed from the chair and caught her up in his arms and held her. Could he ever let her go? When the time came, would he be able to walk away and not look back?

"I needed to feel your arms around me, Dan. I–I love you so much, it hurts. I can't bear to see you go." Pent-up sobs gave way to huge tears. No more being brave!

Her deep sobs broke his heart. He blotted her tears with his fingertips and wanted to cry along with her; his heart was breaking, too. He'd never felt this kind of pain.

She breathed a prayer aloud. "Oh, God, I love him so. Somehow, someway, please work this out. Please, God!"

The two spent the afternoon locked in one another's arms, thinking of what might have been.

❧

At five, Dan bid farewell to the house he'd come to love, and closed the front door behind him for the last time. He and Carlee were silent most of the way to the airport.

The airport was crowded, and for once, the flight was on schedule. They said their farewells surrounded by dozens of strangers.

"I love you, Dan," Carlee repeated as she placed her palms on his cheeks and kissed him for the final time.

"I love you, Carlee," Dan whispered into her ear before he pulled away and entered the walkway.

She stood, waving, as the door closed behind him, separating the two young lovers. He was gone.

❧

Dan phoned her every night the first week. She'd wait by the phone, willing it to ring, longing to hear his voice.

The second week, he phoned only four times. They avoided any discussion about their future. As much as Carlee craved his voice, she knew it was best that they begin to separate from one another. Nothing could come of their three-week romance.

❧

Three days before Christmas, at two o'clock in the morning, Carlee's phone rang, waking her from a fitful sleep. It was Ethel, and she was crying. Jim was experiencing chest pains and she'd called for an ambulance. It was on its way.

Carlee crossed the lawn and arrived the same time as the ambulance. "Oh, Mother Bennett, I'll be there just as soon as I can get Mrs. Grimes here to stay with the children." Carlee shivered in the cold night air as she watched the emergency vehicle rush away down the street.

When she arrived at the hospital, she found the nearly hysterical Ethel in the waiting room. Ethel had been told nothing since they'd arrived except that Jim's condition was very serious. Carlee comforted her mother-in-law as the two women knelt together in prayer and begged the Lord to spare Jim's life.

The doctor came in an hour later. Jim had stabilized some, but it would be awhile before they would know how much damage had been done to his heart. The two women were allowed to go into his room to see him. The sight of all the tubes and machines hooked up to his body frightened them. He looked so ashen-gray and lifeless.

"Call Dan," Ethel said firmly as she placed her hand on her daughter-in-law's arm. "Jim would want him to know."

Carlee rushed to the pay phone and dialed the number Dan had given to her. When his sleepy voice answered with a weak "Hello," she blurted out the news.

A now-wide-awake voice asked, "How bad is he?"

"We don't know. The doctor said it will be some time before they know anything—they're trying to stabilize him."

"I'll catch the next flight and be there in a few hours. Which hospital? How is Ethel doing? Where are the kids?"

"Dan, you can't come. You're in rehearsals!"

"We'll be off over Christmas. I'm coming, Carlee. Stay with Ethel; I'll take a cab from the airport. I love you!"

Built-up stress seemed to flow from her weary body. Dan was coming. And he'd said "I love you."

The next two days were a blur. The three stayed at the hospital most of the time, leaving only long enough to shower and catch a few hours of sleep. Dan was very considerate of Ethel. She told him time and time again how important he had become to her. Her rock to lean on, she called him.

On Christmas Eve, Ethel insisted Carlee and Dan go home and relieve Mrs. Grimes so the children could spend Christmas in their own home. It was nearly midnight before the two finished wrapping gifts, but finally the last present was placed under the tree, ready to be ripped open by two eager children on Christmas morning.

"We'd better hit the sack," Dan said as he bent to kiss Carlee as she sat cross-legged on the floor, surrounded by paper, tape, scissors, and ribbon. He ordered Carlee to bed while he locked up the house and turned out the lights. Soon the house was silent.

She drifted off to sleep quickly, feeling safe and secure. Dan was in the house.

❧

"Look, he's opening his eyes!" Ethel Bennett jumped to her feet and rushed to her husband. "He's squeezing my hand!"

It had been five days since he'd entered the cardiac unit, and other than a few flickers of his eyelids and a slight movement of his hands and legs, he'd shown little response. Carlee joined her mother-in-law beside the bed, and the two women wept for joy and thanked God for a miracle. The doctor had been reluctant to give them any encouragement about Jim making it. It had been obvious, even to the doctors, that God would have to perform a miracle in order for him to survive. And He had!

"I've got to tell Dan," Carlee said softly, so excited it was hard to keep her voice down to a whisper. She wanted to shout praises to the Lord. She rushed into the little waiting room and ran into Dan's open arms. "He's conscious! Oh, Dan, God has answered our prayers—he's going to live!" She buried her head in his chest and clung to him, absorbing his strength.

"He had to make it," Dan said firmly with a jab of his fist into the palm of his other hand. "I need him!"

Carlee thought his words a little strange but never questioned them. She was too happy. And Jim and Dan had become extremely close during their time together.

By the next morning, Jim was able to talk faintly, even laugh, but he still was very weak. "I knew you were here,

Dan—I could hear all three of you."

Dan quit smiling. It pained him deeply to think how close they'd come to losing Jim. Jim had become like a father to him, in ways Carlee knew nothing about. He'd spent many hours at the rink with Jim during the time she'd been at home with the children—hours she'd thought he'd spent with his parents.

❧

The week between Christmas Day and New Year's Day was a busy time for the rink, but the rink was the last thing on Carlee's mind, or on Ethel's. Jim and his recovery came first, but she was concerned about Dan and his rehearsals, too.

"Don't worry about it," he assured her when they finally got down to talking about when he might leave and go back to Florida. "I'm a fast learner."

"Dan, you don't have to stay. Jim is getting better every day. They're going to move him to intermediate care tomorrow. Ethel and I can handle things here—you'd better go." It pained her to voice those last words. She didn't want him to go—ever! She'd said good-bye to him once already, and their second farewell would be no easier.

Later that afternoon he sat in a chair in the corner of the hospital room, staring out the window. He and Jim had similar backgrounds. But Jim had the one thing in his life Dan didn't have—a personal relationship with God.

❧

Once dinner was over and the dishes done, Carlee turned back the quilt on the bed in Bobby's room and suggested that Dan get some well-deserved rest. He would be taking the midnight to seven A.M. shift at the hospital, then flying back to Florida. He grabbed her wrist as she turned to leave the bedroom. "Don't go. Please!"

She allowed herself to be pulled onto the bed, next to Dan, and found her heart racing wildly at his touch.

"I have to be near you, Carlee. This is my last chance. Stay with me," he begged, his eyes pleading with her.

She drew back, knowing her weakness.

He quickly raised up and propped himself on one elbow. "No, I didn't mean that the way it sounded. I just want you here till I fall asleep, that's all."

Her cheeks flared with pink and she felt foolish to have misunderstood the meaning of his words. Dan had never said or done anything improper; he'd never asked her to compromise, and of course he wouldn't do it now.

"I'll stay," she said softly as she lowered herself back onto the bed beside him and pushed the hair from his forehead. For nearly an hour they talked, but eventually sleep overtook him and he drifted off. She'd been blessed with this kind of love twice in her lifetime. But like Robert, he was being taken away from her. She sat there watching him, praying for him, once more asking the Lord to let them be together.

When she awoke, the bed in Bobby's room was empty and a note was propped against the basket of silk flowers on the kitchen table. He'd gone to the hospital to relieve Ethel.

&

Carlee and the children were waiting when Dan arrived at eight A.M. to pick Carlee up. He waved to the two tearstained faces with their forced smiles as he backed the car into the street and headed toward the airport. Carlee moved as close to Dan as she could get, took his hand, and wound her fingers tightly through his. He swallowed hard and kept his eyes on the road.

After parking in the short-term parking lot, he grabbed his bags from the trunk and walked alongside Carlee into the terminal. They selected two chairs in the corner and settled down for their final few minutes together. Dan pulled her close and rubbed his cheek against hers as he'd done so many times before. Suddenly he laughed aloud. "I wonder how many of my so-called friends would believe that I could be so in love with a woman and, in all this time, all I've ever done is hold her and kiss her?" He cupped her chin and lifted her face toward his. "To some, lovemaking means sex. They only think they know love. Carlee, with you I've discovered what true love is, and we have it, dearest. They don't have a clue!"

A feeling of pride flowed though her. Living by God's standards was worth it after all. Dan respected her.

"I don't know how, I don't know when, but someday, Carlee Bennett, we're going to figure this thing out. I want you to be my wife—in every way. I want to be Bobby's and Becca's dad. I know you know how to get answers from God. Please, ask Him to work this out because I love you, Carlee Bennett. You're my life!"

Surely God would work out their problems. Dan was so open. He'd even asked her to pray; that had to be a sign from heaven. Her hope for the two of them was renewed, rekindled by Dan's declaration of love and request for prayer.

The flight to Florida was announced, and he walked out of her life for a second painful time.

seventeen

On the last day of January, Jim Bennett walked into his house with the aid of a cane. He was on the mend. It'd been a rough month for Carlee. Managing the rink without him was no easy task, but she had to keep up a facade for the sake of the children and for Jim Bennett. She couldn't let them know how tired she was and how much she was hurting.

February came and went. Dan called at least four times a week and they'd talk for hours. He begged Carlee to come to California to see the new show, but with Jim's physical condition so fragile, she knew such a trip would be impossible.

The first week in March, Jim gathered his little troop of staunch backers and told them, "We need to pray." He took his wife's hand in his and reached for Carlee's. "Lord. I thank You for sparing my life. And I thank You for each member of my family. You know, Lord, what I am about to tell them. Help me to say it, and help them accept it."

All eyes turned toward the man they respected and adored. What was he going to tell them?

Jim took a deep breath and looked around the circle at each one before he spoke. He turned to his wife first. "Ethel. You've been the perfect wife. You've stood by me through thick and thin." He patted his slightly rounded tummy. "Mostly thick," he added with a hollow laugh.

Next, he turned to his daughter-in-law, his only son's wife, whom he loved as a daughter. "Carlee, you've been the daughter we never had. We've loved you as much as if you'd been born to us. Our son loved you with all his heart. And we know you loved him with that same kind of love. It hasn't been easy,

159

but you never complained."

"But, Father Bennett, what are you—"

He held up a hand for silence, then grinned at the two little ones, his pride and joy. .

"Bobby, you're the image of your dad. The Lord must have put you here to take his place in our hearts. I'm proud of you."

"What about me, Grandpa?" Becca asked, her eyes shining expectantly.

The man nodded his head, then lifted his face heavenward. "Ah, yes. Becca. My shining light! I'm as proud of you as I am of Bobby."

"Jim?" Ethel asked with a glow of love in her voice as she slipped her hand in his. "What are you trying to say?"

He rubbed his eyes with his hankie, then stuffed it into his pocket. "I have a confession to make. I haven't been completely honest with you about what the doctor said to me."

"Jim!" Ethel's hand moved to her mouth. "What? What are you saying?"

"Whoa, Mother. I'm not going to die. At least not now. Not from my heart attack. But the doctor has said I *may* die if I don't change my lifestyle." He swallowed hard. "I've made a major decision; I've decided to sell the rink!"

"But Father Bennett, I can run the rink; I've been doing it since Christmas," Carlee argued, knowing how much the rink meant to her father-in-law. "Please don't sell it. We can manage, somehow!"

"No, Carlee," he said firmly. "You can't. The children need you. I've watched you push yourself these past few months. It's too much for one woman, especially when she has a family who needs her."

"But," she pleaded, "we could hire a permanent manager."

Jim shook his head. "No, I've thought it over, weighed all the pros and cons, and selling the rink is the only thing that makes sense. I've already contacted some interested parties;

they're checking into it right now."

The two women made no further argument. How could they? Jim was right. To keep the rink would only prolong their predicament. His good health was the most important thing to both of them. Nothing should stand in the way of that.

Carlee unburdened her heart to Dan when he called that night. He listened, but as with their own situation, he offered no solutions.

She lay awake till the wee hours of the morning, feeling overwhelmed. Was God forsaking her? Didn't He care? Didn't He understand?

On Carlee's birthday, the UPS man delivered a cumbersome box, addressed to Carlee Bennett. There, packed among hundreds of foam pellets, was the newest collector Barbie doll. There was no card inside, but she didn't need one to know who'd sent the beautiful doll. Dan!

"Hey, how'd the birthday party go?" he asked when she phoned him that evening to thank him for her present. His question puzzled her. Ethel had given her an impromptu surprise party the night before, but how could he have known?

Later that evening, Jim Bennett called another family meeting, this time to inform them about the buyer he had for the rink. "We've already done the paperwork—the closing will be Monday, and the new owner will take over on Tuesday."

"So soon?" Carlee stared at her father-in-law. He hadn't said a thing to her about having a firm buyer. And they'd already signed the paperwork? The sale would close in just four days; she'd have to hustle to get her office in order and be ready to vacate the premises.

When Dan phoned, she filled him in on all the details as she knew them. "It's all happened so fast, Dan."

"How do you feel about this, sweetheart?" His voice was filled with concern. "I know you love that rink."

She sat cross-legged in the middle of the bed and stared at Dan's picture on the nightstand. "I loved it more when you were here. I miss you so much."

He let out a slow sigh. "At least then I won't have to worry about you so much. I wish I knew how to pray like Jim; I'd pray for you when I wake up early and think about you."

Dan wished he knew how to pray? Like Jim? *Oh, Lord God. Did I understand him correctly? Is all of this what it's going to take to get Dan into Your family?* Pushing down the joy that sprang up within her, she instructed him gently, "God is ready to listen, even early in the morning, Dan. He doesn't want eloquent words. Just words from our hearts. He's always ready to listen."

"Ummm. In that case, I may give it a try," he teased.

⁂

The day the sale of the rink closed, Jim asked Carlee and the children to join them for supper. Ethel fixed his favorites: fried chicken, mashed potatoes, and strawberry shortcake.

The table was set for the five of them. Jim looked at the beautifully appointed table, then went to the china cabinet and took out another plate, cup, and saucer and placed them on the table with the five already there. "Better get another glass, and a napkin, and more silverware, Ethel," he said to his wife with a mischievous grin. "We have company coming for dinner."

"Jim!" Ethel said accusingly as she scurried to set the sixth place at the table. "Why didn't you tell me?"

"Who's coming, Grandpa?" Becca asked.

Jim smiled with pride, as if he'd pulled off the caper of the century. "The rink's new owner, Becca."

"You invited him here?" Ethel asked in surprise. "To have dinner with us? Isn't that going a bit far? Giving up the rink has got to be hard for you."

The doorbell rang as the five Bennetts stood staring at one

another. Apparently their guest had arrived. "I'll get it!" Jim stated with authority. It was more of a command than an offer. "Why don't you all take a seat in the living room? I'll make the introductions there."

The two women and two children sat side by side on the tapestry sofa and waited. They could hear muffled voices in the hall. Perhaps Father Bennett was warning the new owner that the family hadn't been informed about his coming until the last minute.

Jim moved into the archway between the two rooms and leaned on his cane. "Family," he said with one of the broadest smiles they'd ever seen on his handsome face, "I want you to meet the new owner of the Ice Palace." He stood back and motioned toward the front hall as majestically as if he were heralding a king.

All eyes focused expectantly on the doorway as the new owner stepped into view. Four people gasped in unison as Jim reached for his guest's hand and drew him into the room.

"Troops, I'd like to present the new owner of the rink— Dan Castleberry!"

There stood Dan with a smile as broad as Jim's. The four sat glued to the sofa with their mouths dangling open. Surely they were dreaming. Could this be possible? Could Dan really be the new owner?

Jim shoved Dan toward them with his free hand while he leaned on the cane with the other. "Well, are you going to welcome our guest? Or just sit there and stare?"

Carlee flew into Dan's waiting arms. "Is this true, Dan? Are you the new owner?" She pushed back to search his face. "It can't be true. But if not, what are you doing here?"

He pulled her close and held her fast as Jim moved to stand by Ethel and the children. "It's true, Carlee. I'm here to stay. If you'll have me." He flooded her face with kisses as her in-laws looked on, smiling with approval.

"But, how? I don't under—"

Jim Bennett dropped onto the sofa and pulled his wife down beside him. "Dan, let me explain. I'm kinda proud of my part in all of this. Not every day I get to play Cupid."

Dan nodded as he dropped into the recliner and pulled Carlee onto his lap, along with two wiggling children.

"Dan and I had many interesting talks when he was here those first three weeks. He came over to the rink a number of times and we'd talk about a lot of things. Dan is a fine young man. He'd put his personal life on hold while he worked on his career." He nodded toward Ethel, who nodded back as she patted her husband's hand. "I certainly could identify with that. His career was everything to him—that is, until he met our Carlee!" He winked at his daughter-in-law.

"Dan confided in me that he loved Carlee so deeply that he was considering giving up his skating with Ice Fantasy. I could understand that; I'd made that same decision when I met Ethel years ago!" He gave his wife an adoring grin. "However, that wasn't the only problem Dan and Carlee had. Carlee was a Christian—she had values and standards Dan didn't understand. Not that he disagreed with them, mind you, he just didn't understand her relationship with God. He'd never experienced it himself."

He aimed his cane at Carlee. "Carlee, on the other hand, had decided to put God first in her life when she was a child. That relationship has been the most important one in her life. More important than what she had with our Robert. And more important than her relationship with Dan."

He pointed the tip of the cane in Dan's direction. "Now, Robert was a Christian, too. So, no problem for them on that count. But it was different with Dan. He made no claim about God. That hurt Carlee; she'd promised God she'd never be unequally yoked to an unbeliever."

Carlee pursed her lips. What he was saying was absolutely

true, but she'd never voiced it quite that strongly to Dan. Now, she wished she had.

"I knew these two were meant to be together the moment I met Dan. So did Ethel." Ethel nodded.

"So I said to myself, I've got to work on that boy—explain God to him. And I did! I asked the Lord to send Dan to me if it was God's will and if I was supposed to talk to him. And, sure enough, Dan showed up at the rink while Carlee was home with the kids."

Carlee lifted Dan's chin with her palm. "I didn't know you spent time with Father Bennett. Why didn't you tell me?"

" 'Cause he wasn't ready, that's why! The timing wasn't right," Jim interjected. "Well, to go on with my story; Dan left for Florida and I asked the Lord, 'Where did I go wrong?' You two weren't any closer than you'd been a week after he got here. I asked for another chance to talk to Dan and the Lord gave it to me. I had a heart attack! The Lord answers in strange ways, believe me. Tell her, Dan."

Dan straightened himself in his chair, smiled at Jim, and took up where Jim left off. "Jim and I spent many hours together at the hospital. We talked about my long-range career goal to own my own rink someday and to be its pro. When the doctor told Jim he had to give up the rink or die, he remembered what I'd said. So—he called me!"

"Dan reminded me that buying the rink and moving to Kansas City would only solve half their problem—there was this thing standing between them about knowing God," Jim added.

Dan beamed at Carlee. "So, Jim said to me, 'That's no problem. Just say yes to God!' I said, 'You mean it's that simple? That's all I have to do?' He read a few Scriptures, and I suddenly got it! I knew I was a sinner and I needed a Savior. God's plan of salvation was so simple, even I could understand it, with Jim's help." He gave a slight laugh, then became serious.

"I finally realized I had to ask God's forgiveness. I knelt in my room right there while I was on the phone, and I confessed my sin and asked God's forgiveness and asked Him to be Lord of my life." Big tears formed in his eyes but he made no attempt to hide them. "Carlee, I've been born again. Now I know what John 5:24 means, and I've taken it as my life's verse." He touched her face as tears flowed down his cheeks.

Carlee spoke with difficulty through tears of joy as her eyes searched his. "Oh, Dan, God has answered my prayer. But why didn't you tell me? You knew I'd been praying for you."

He wiped her tears away with his hankie. "We decided to keep it a secret between the two of us, to make sure the sale would work out first. So that no one would be disappointed."

"That's how you knew about my birthday party!" Carlee stated. "You two talked on the phone that night, right?"

Dan nodded. "Uh-huh. I almost spilled the beans."

She nuzzled his hair with her chin as she and her two children snuggled close to the security and warmth of his body. "But, Dan! How could you afford to buy the rink? I know the Bennetts are depending on the profits to take care of their living expenses for the rest of their lives. That rink has been their livelihood. Did your parents help?"

He laughed aloud. "My parents? Help me buy a skating rink? Forget it! I wouldn't even ask. No; I did it without them. They don't even know about it yet." He stroked her hair lovingly. "Carlee, I've saved every penny I could during the ten years I've been with the ice show."

"Except for the money you've frittered away on expensive Barbie dolls?" she chided with a playful jab to his ribs.

"Yep, except for that. My aunt set up a trust fund for me when I was a baby. That and the interest it's drawn, along with what I've saved and what my grandmother left me, was almost enough. Fortunately, I have a prospective father-in-law who was willing to take a chance on me and carry the remainder. Right, Jim?"

"You bet! I know a sure thing when I see it," Jim Bennett said proudly as he peered at the happy couple.

"I still don't understand, Dan. Ice Fantasy? What are you going to do about that? They're counting on you!"

"All taken care of, kiddo. When Jim contacted me, I immediately went to Tom and told him I was buying the rink. I told him how much I loved you and how I wanted to spend my life with you and the kids."

Jim broke in. "He said, 'Go for it!' Right, Dan?"

Dan nodded. "Right! He brought in the lead skater from our show that's been touring Europe. I worked with him day and night and taught him all my routines. That's why I haven't called you as often as I'd have liked. No time! He's already taken my place in the new show."

She lifted her eyebrows questioningly.

"Beginning tomorrow!" Dan answered her unspoken question before she could ask it. "I'm here to stay."

It was more than Carlee could comprehend.

"Got any other problems you want solved? I'm your man!" Jim was happy to take every ounce of credit he could get.

Carlee slipped from Dan's lap and hugged him. "Nope, you old softy. You've solved them all. You're wonderful, Father Bennett. The best father-in-law a girl could have."

"Well, I have one more problem. A major one!" Dan warned from his place in the recliner.

The hugging came to a halt as three adults faced Dan. What other problem could there be?

"Only you can solve it, Carlee," he said as he crossed the room and pulled the love of his life from Jim's arms and into his own. "I haven't asked you to marry me. Not officially." He held her hand and dramatically dropped to one knee. "Carlee. I've already asked your father-in-law for permission, but I haven't asked you. Will you marry me?"

The overcome young mother reached down and kissed the lips of the man she'd loved since that very first day they'd met. The man she'd prayed for so many times. "I wish I could find the right words to express my love for you, Dan. This is the happiest day of my life. Of course I'll marry you!" She smothered him with kisses as two confused children watched, not sure what was happening.

"Then this is for you, dearest," he said as he unbuttoned the breast pocket of his shirt. "I was hoping you'd say 'yes,' so I brought this with me. My grandmother's ring." He took her left hand in his and slipped the lovely ring on her finger. It fit perfectly. "I love you, Carlee, and I promise, with our God as my witness, that I'll love you and care for you till death do us part."

Becca's tiny hands tugged on his pant leg. "Dan, I love you, too; where's my ring?" They all laughed as Becca smiled, not sure why her words were so amusing.

Dan gathered his prospective family around him and enfolded them in his arms. "Actually," he said as he looked at each member of the precious little family he was claiming as his own, "I'm asking all three of you to marry me. What do you say?"

"Fine with me!" Bobby proclaimed quickly as he shook Dan's hand, eager to turn over his title of "man of the house" to this man he'd grown to love.

"I'll marry with you, Dan," Becca said as she hugged his neck and tangled her fingers in his hair.

His eyes met Carlee's. "And you, my love? Will you promise to spend the rest of your life with me?"

"Yes! Oh, yes! A thousand times, yes!" Carlee threw herself into Dan's arms. "I love you, Dan Castleberry. God has given us our miracle!"

epilogue

The day before Christmas, a big truck pulled into the rink's parking lot and carefully positioned itself. Its long crane cautiously lifted the giant sign and eased it toward the waiting steel poles. Two workmen standing in a cherry picker perched high overhead grabbed the sign and guided it toward the waiting platform where it would rest until welded in place.

Dan Castleberry and his wife leaned against the building and watched the process. Two children squealed and ran figure-eights around their legs as Jim and Ethel Bennett watched from the comfort of two folding chairs their new son-in-law had placed next to the building, where they could watch in safety.

"You feeling okay?" Dan asked his bride of six months as he pulled her into the warmth of his arms, with love and concern shining on his face for all to see.

"We're both fine!" she answered as she spread her fingers wide across her tummy and patted it gently.

"God has been so good to us, sweetheart." Dan placed his fingers over hers and nestled his face into her neck. "Think it's a boy?" He lifted her hand to his lips and tenderly kissed her fingertips.

She gazed into eyes filled with pride. "I hope so. I want to call him Daniel. After you, my husband."

"Mama! Daddy! Look; the sign is up!" Bobby shouted as he pointed to the magnificent new sign resting on its sturdy posts in front of the newly remodeled ice rink.

"What's it say, Daddy?" Becca asked as she ran to Dan and leaped into his arms.

169

He held his little daughter in one arm and hugged his wife with the other, as his son stood beside him with a skinny arm wrapped around his waist.

"Ice Castle, Becca. Ice Castle!"

A Letter To Our Readers

Dear Reader:

In order that we might better contribute to your reading enjoyment, we would appreciate your taking a few minutes to respond to the following questions. We welcome your comments and read each form and letter we receive. When completed, please return to the following:

Rebecca Germany, Fiction Editor
Heartsong Presents
PO Box 719
Uhrichsville, Ohio 44683

1. Did you enjoy reading *Ice Castle?*
   ☐ Very much. I would like to see more books
      by this author!
   ☐ Moderately
      I would have enjoyed it more if _____

   _____

   _____

2. Are you a member of **Heartsong Presents**? Yes ☐ No ☐
   If no, where did you purchase this book?_____

   _____

3. How would you rate, on a scale from 1 (poor) to 5 (superior), the cover design?_____

4. On a scale from 1 (poor) to 10 (superior), please rate the following elements.

   _____ Heroine   _____ Plot

   _____ Hero   _____ Inspirational theme

   _____ Setting   _____ Secondary characters

5. These characters were special because_____

_____

_____

6. How has this book inspired your life?_____

_____

_____

7. What settings would you like to see covered in future **Heartsong Presents** books?_____

_____

_____

8. What are some inspirational themes you would like to see treated in future books?_____

_____

_____

9. Would you be interested in reading other **Heartsong Presents** titles?   Yes ❑   No ❑

10. Please check your age range:
    ❑ Under 18   ❑ 18-24   ❑ 25-34
    ❑ 35-45   ❑ 46-55   ❑ Over 55

11. How many hours per week do you read?_____

Name _____

Occupation _____

Address _____

City _____ State _____ Zip _____

This heartwarming collection of short stories is perfect

for "want to" readers—those big on reading but short on time. From the story of an engaged couple looking for common ground amongst their dissimilarities to the account of a single mother's thoughts as her daughter desires to meet the father who left them, this collection of inspirational short stories is sometimes lighthearted, sometimes humorous, and often poignant. Focusing on the joys and heartaches of love—romantic love, love for family members, love between friends, even the love of an elderly gentleman for his pets—*Short Stories for Long Rainy Days* will bring gentle smiles, soft chuckles, and even a few tears as readers experience the manifold facets of love. 224 pages, Hardbound, 5" x 7"

··Hearts♥ng··

HEARTSONG PRESENTS *TITLES AVAILABLE NOW:*

········Presents········

Great Inspirational Romance at a Great Price!

Heartsong Presents books are inspirational romances in contemporary and historical settings, designed to give you an enjoyable, spirit-lifting reading experience. You can choose wonderfully written titles from some of today's best authors like Veda Boyd Jones, Yvonne Lehman, Tracie Peterson, Debra White Smith, and many others.

When ordering quantities less than twelve, above titles are $2.95 each.
Not all titles may be available at time of order.